SEXY CLAUS

THE NAUGHTY LIST SERIES

MELLANIE SZERETO

amatoria press

BOOKS BY MELLANIE SZERETO

The Homegrown Café Book Club series ~

Makin' Bacon

The Farmer Takes a Husband

The Butcher and the Baker

When Harry Met Wally

And Baby Makes 2½

The Homegrown Café Book Club Boxed Set

Love on the Menu series ~

Love Served Hot

Red Hot Pepper

Hot Tamale Nights (coming soon)

Love on the Menu...Extra Hot standalones ~

Just Desserts

Iced Latté

A Little Appetizer

The Main Dish

Dressing on the Side

Flavor of the Day

Love on the Menu…Steamed trilogy ~

Egging Her On

Sweetening Her Up

Reeling Her In

Love on the Menu: Steamed Boxed Set

Nerds & Babies series ~

The Nerd Next Door

The Nerd Upstairs

The Nerd Downstairs

Nerds & Babies Collection

Nerd Love series ~

Comma Kaze

Comma Sutra (coming soon)

Romancing the Phone series ~

Call Me…Maybe

Smooth Operator

Hang-Ups (coming soon)

Telephone Lines (2025)

Dialed Up (2026)

Mixed Messages (2026)

The Jerk Series ~

Jerk in the Box

Jerk of All Trades

Small Town Jerk

Jerk the Ripper

Two Forks Hollow Christmas short story series ~

Snowballed

Two Nights Before Christmas

Mistletoe Miscalculation

Sexy Claus (Creekside 1) also part of The Naughty List series

Roll With It (Creekside 2)

Standalone Short Stories & Novellas ~

Behind the Mask ~ contemporary romance

Death Benefits ~ paranormal romance

Diner 49er ~ contemporary romcom

Divorce Actually ~ contemporary romcom

Frostbite ~ contemporary holiday romcom

G Marks the Spot ~ contemporary romcom

Karma-lized ~ contemporary romcom

Kiss My Sass ~ contemporary romcom

Mad About You ~ romantic suspense

Mom I'd Love to Marry ~ contemporary romance

Not Quite Cupid ~ contemporary romcom

With Bells On ~ contemporary romcom

You Had Me at Goodbye ~ contemporary romcom

The Sextet Anthologies ~

Volume 1: Sharing

Volume 2: Dirty Dancing

Volume 3: Occupational Hazards

Volume 4: Entanglements

Volume 5: Mistletoe & Ménage

The Sextet Presents standalones ~

Playing in the Raine: A Toy Story

Bound by Voodoo: Legends

CHAPTER ONE

CHRISTY RIME PASTED ON A PERKY SMILE AND WEDGED THE potted plant from her desk into the box on her chair. Once she packed the last of her office belongings, she planned to swing by the coffee shop for a peppermint tea and hit the road—again.

"Are you sure you don't want a piece of cheesecake to take with you?" Her ex-fiancé's new wife—one of her now-former co-workers—stood at the entrance to the cubicle Christy had called home for the last two years.

"No, thanks. I don't have any way to keep it cold while I'm traveling." Cherry topping definitely wasn't her favorite, although she had no intention of telling the kind people who'd gone to the trouble of throwing her a going-away party this afternoon.

"I wish you weren't leaving, but I totally get why you need to go. I'm really sorry about...everything. And your dad, of course." Julie's remorse shone as much in her teary eyes as her frown.

Shaking off the unnecessary sympathy, Christy slid an unopened package of encouragement cards, an emery board, and a stress ball in the hole next to the potted succulents. Then she dropped the handful of outdated business cards into the recycle can and gave her space a final scan. "It's okay. Really. I'm happy for you and James."

Hopefully, the vague reference to her feelings would be enough to keep her arm's-length friend from delving any deeper into the feelings about her estranged father's death.

Julie swiped a tear from her cheek and rushed forward, engulfing Christy in a hug. "Keep in touch. Promise?"

An outright yes required follow-through, which wasn't something she had ever felt compelled to do when she'd moved on to a new job in a new town. The past belonged behind her, and she'd become an expert at putting that skill to good use long ago. "I'll try to let you know when I get settled again, but I'm not sure when that'll be. Lots of details to take care of."

"Okay." After one more gentle pat, Julie released her and stepped into the corridor that bordered the wall of not-quite offices. "Safe travels and happy adventures."

Relief at the other woman's wistful smile and graceful wave sparked a twinge of regret as Christy hefted the box. She headed toward the elevator in the opposite direction. As much as she bore Julie and James no ill will, an escape without any prolonged goodbyes would make life considerably more bearable.

A chilly blast of mid-December air chased her to her car, reminding her of the canceled beach vacation she'd originally planned for the holidays. Instead of basking in the sun and surf, she had to meet with a lawyer to discuss a will, clean out her childhood home, and enlist the help of a real estate agent to put the house on the market. Then, and only then, could she finally cut all her ties to the town where she'd been born and raised.

Memories invaded her mind as she drove northeast, and not even the traffic on I-71 through Columbus and the calming scent of her tea distracted her from the pointless thoughts. Her father's fibs and omissions didn't matter. The truth might have hurt, but the big lie had burdened her with far more guilt than a child could handle or deserved.

The boyfriend she'd walked away from didn't matter, either. Staying hadn't been a mentally workable option for her, and he'd made the choice not to go with her. She had also lost the friend she'd loved that day—her best friend, her rock —the day he'd told her he couldn't leave.

Wouldn't.

No one ever chose her for the long term, but she'd given up on any kind of expectations of permanence—even before James had fallen instantly and madly in love with her co-worker two months after his marriage proposal. He was hardly the first. She should've said no, knowing the engagement wouldn't last. Unfortunately, her DNA and upbringing had taught her to be agreeable to a fault.

A helper.

Ha. More like a happy little doormat.

No more. No more being a placeholder until something better comes along and no more trying to solve other people's problems—except in the office.

Not that I have an office at the moment.

She would never regret helping her clients relearn how to navigate the world after life-altering injuries and illnesses, but she hadn't researched her future prospects yet. Her next move would certainly be after the first of the year, especially since she had no idea how long handling all the details in her hometown would take.

Dusk quickly morphed into darkness, lit up by headlights, taillights, and the occasional exit with a smattering of signs and streetlights. Christmas decorations outlined a house or barn here and there, but the holiday spirit had deserted her years ago. Indifference had settled in and made itself comfortable during the two and a half decades of being on her own.

Her neck and shoulders tensed and her stomach knotted before the next big green sign came into focus.

Creekside. 10 miles.

Though she'd avoided this area of Ohio since leaving it at eighteen, her body and her brain somehow recognized it, even in the dark. After a right turn from the off-ramp and several miles down the county road, she would need to take a left at the big red barn and follow that road into town.

Her flight response kicked in, urging her to continue past the exit, but delaying the inevitable would only prolong her obligations.

Closure.

It was the only positive aspect of returning home.

No. Not home.

Creekside hadn't been home since her eighteenth birthday.

She focused on the painted lines as the pavement ascended the ramp to the stop sign and then guided her away from the interstate. Each curve, dip, and rise seemed familiar, like she'd driven the same route yesterday or last week.

Muscle memory.

She used the technique to teach her clients new ways to do tasks they'd done easily during the "before" times. Repetition trained the body and mind to work together. Would the day ever come that she lived long enough in a new town again to build a new neural pathway as strong as this one?

Multicolored twinkles lit up the roofline, eaves, and corners of a large structure not far ahead, bringing her full attention back to the road. Her insides spun and whirled at the sight. How many times had she seen the same outline during her childhood?

Too many to count.

How many holidays had her father sent her to her grand-parents' house?

All of them.

Shoving the feelings into the imaginary box she'd created long ago, she flipped on her turn signal. Hopefully, once she nailed this door to the past shut, it wouldn't haunt her anymore.

I can do this. Nobody even has to know I'm here.

A faint glow illuminated the lowest part of the sky in front of her, announcing her imminent arrival as much as the REDUCED SPEED AHEAD sign and the new-to-her WELCOME TO CREEKSIDE stone marker.

She slowed to the new speed limit as she passed a farm equipment store that hadn't existed when she'd lived here. Most of the homes beyond it were decorated for Christmas, as were the businesses now sprawled a few blocks farther from downtown than they used to be. A mix of cars, trucks, and SUVs filled the high school parking lot, and a pair of school buses from a neighboring town stood out in the drop-off and pickup lanes near the side entrance.

A Friday night basketball game, no doubt.

At least fewer people would be out and about when she walked to the closest restaurant for carryout after checking into the hotel. The slimmer the chances of running into someone she'd known, the better for her state of mind. Her appointment with the lawyer tomorrow morning was going to be stressful enough.

Light-up snowflakes hung from the utility poles for more than half a dozen blocks, replacing the ringing-bell design from her childhood. Not unexpectedly, some storefronts had changed and others had stayed the same. Creekside's business district looked like any other small town in Ohio, with its mix of old brick buildings with second-floor offices or apartments and newer construction that housed restaurants and other small businesses.

Finally spotting the hotel three blocks away, she exhaled to ease some of the tension radiating through her neck and shoulders. A quiet meal in her room might let her come close to relaxing.

Almost there.

The next stoplight turned yellow, even though no cars waited at the side street. As she stopped, a bundled form in a wheelchair slowly rolled down the ramp from the sidewalk into the crosswalk. Gloved hands pushed forward on the wheels, but the progress was slow. About a third of the way across, the chair's front wheel dropped into a pothole, sparking annoyance and an ache in Christy's chest.

"What good is a crosswalk if it's impassable and unsafe?" She shoved the gearshift into park, turned on her hazard lights, and shut off the engine. Tugging up her collar, she hurried toward the middle of the intersection.

A frustrated growl accompanied an ineffective attempt to dislodge the wheel. "Damn it!"

Making sure she was well within the rider's peripheral vision, Christy paused. "Looks like the town needs to do some repair work on the road. Would you like some help?"

Rather than answer, the woman dropped her hands from the rims and lowered her chin to her chest. "It's not like I have a choice. I'm blocking the lane, and I can't do this by myself. I just want to go home."

A surge of compassion melded with the automatic switch to therapist mode. "You could if there wasn't a hole where you're trying to go. Have you learned how to do a pop-up? I can spot you if you need help."

"A pop-up?" Blue eyes met her gaze as wavy brown hair fell away from the young woman's face. "You know how to drive this thing? I tried to learn, but going straight and around corners on a smooth surface is all I can do after three months of practicing. My hands are too sore to do anything else. And don't even get me started on my back. I feel like I've aged a hundred years since the accident. I'm probably never going to walk again, and the insurance is waffling on whether or not they'll pay for an electric model."

"I absolutely understand your frustration. We can talk about the insurance stuff after we get you unstuck if you want to." Christy crouched down to eye-level and offered a smile she actually felt for the first time today. "I'm an occupational therapist. I've learned how to do everything my wheelchair clients need to know, including wheelies. Since you're new at this, I can talk you through it and be your spotter."

"But…" Her unofficial student glanced past her and back again. "What about your car? You can't just leave it parked in the middle of the street."

"My flashers are on, and everybody else who comes along can sit and wait. We're going to make sure you're able to get across the street safely." She cast quick glances in both directions and straightened. "All clear. Are you ready for your first lesson?"

"Um, okay. I guess." The young woman's hesitation spoke volumes about her wavering confidence. "So…I really appreciate you stopping. The guy who was my occupational therapist moved out of state this week, and most people are pretty awkward around me now. I'm Brenna."

"It's very nice to meet you, Brenna. I'm Christy." She extended her hand, glad she'd stopped to offer her support.

"I'm only in town temporarily, but I'm happy to help while I'm here or until you have someone else lined up. Hands on the wheels like this."

Guiding her new acquaintance through the proper motions to lift her front wheels, Christy savored the chance to be useful during her forced hiatus from the career she loved. Several tries later, they finally reached the sidewalk on the opposite side of the street.

Thick wisps of fog in front of Brenna revealed the physical effort she'd exerted. "Will that ever be easy for me?"

"Easy? Maybe. Easier? Yes, with practice. That you were open to trying is something to be proud of. Not everyone wants to."

A small smile transformed the young woman's face, but she seemed at a loss for words.

Christy's stomach rumbled under her wool peacoat, nudging her to move along, but her feet refused to budge. "I haven't eaten yet, and there's a pizza place right here. Would you like to join me?"

"Are you sure that's okay? I mean, yes, I would, but you don't have to feel obligated." Brenna's skin flushed a deeper shade of pink around the cold-induced color on her nose and cheeks. "Their breadsticks are my favorite."

Snuffing out a small flame of anger at whoever had excluded Brenna because of her disability, intentional or not, Christy grinned. "Yum. I love breadsticks. I'll meet you there in a few minutes."

Before her new friend could change her mind, Christy hustled back to her car. By the time she started the engine and switched off the flashers, a pickup truck and an SUV sat behind her.

Honk. I dare you.

Surprisingly, neither driver laid on their horn.

She'd been so focused on helping Brenna that she had no idea how long they'd been waiting. She flipped on her turn signal, lowered her window, and waved her hand at the people who'd been patient. Did they recognize their wheelchair resident and respect her right to use crosswalks and sidewalks like anyone else?

Christy pulled into an empty parking space as Brenna rolled toward the entrance to the restaurant. Though her progress across the lot was fairly slow, she clearly didn't plan to give up.

As promised, Christy met her in time to pull open and hold the door—that didn't have an automatic opener. The threshold wasn't exactly chair-friendly, either, but her companion managed enough of a wheelie to navigate the bump while Christy stood at the ready to assist, without being obvious. "What's good here, besides the breadsticks?"

"My dad always orders the lasagna special, but I like their margherita pizza. And I usually get a house salad." Reaching into her crossbody purse, Brenna pulled out her phone. "Speaking of Dad, I should text him and let him know where I am. He worries."

After an acknowledging nod and a scan of the dining room layout, Christy stepped up to the hostess stand. "A regular table for two please. No high-top or booth. In a corner would be great, if you have it."

The young man retrieved a pair of menus from the lower shelf. "Yes, ma'am. This way."

She gestured for Brenna to go first and trailed along behind her. When they stopped at the table, Christy motioned to the side with the best access. "Can you please remove this chair?"

His confused expression became a blush, signaling his

realization that one of his patrons had brought her own seat. "Oh, sure. Your server will be right out."

As soon as they'd settled in, Brenna heaved a breathy sigh. "Thanks for handling that. Dad and I haven't done dine-in since before the accident. It always sounded like too much work, but you... I don't want to put anybody out because I need special—"

"You have just as much right to be here as anyone else. People request tables be moved together for large groups and chairs taken away to make room for highchairs. All kinds of things like that. Having access isn't special treatment. Asking for what you need can be hard at first, but most people and places will accommodate you. And you're allowed to complain if they don't, just like you'd complain about mediocre service, dirty silverware and plates, or bad food." Christy slid her menu to the edge of the table, keeping her tone conversational, even though a lack of accessibility always sparked her temper. "Margherita is one of my favorites, so why don't you order? My treat, by the way, since I invited you."

Brenna seemed to finally relax by the time the waiter arrived. After he dropped off their drinks, her phone buzzed. She shook her head and frowned before she tapped in a response. "My dad is freaking out that I left the basketball game without telling him. He said to stay where I am and he'll be here to pick me up in fifteen minutes. I told him thirty minutes, or I'll cause a scene. He hated the drama when I was a teenager, not that I acted like a brat often."

Her giggle assured Christy the young woman across from her was going to be a pleasure to work with for the four to six weeks dealing with the house would take. "If you don't mind me asking, how old are you?"

"Twenty-four." Brenna raised her chin, like she was

trying to muster a bit of courage. She paused while the server delivered their order. Her smile faded a bit as she continued. "I've felt more like my grandma's age since the accident."

"Some days, I feel like I could be a thousand. Life can be...challenging. Physically and emotionally." Determined not to let either of them get sucked into a pointless wasteland of self-pity and misery, Christy plated a slice for them both. "But pizza helps. I hope it tastes as good as it looks and smells."

The distraction seemed to work on her supper companion since she grinned and added a breadstick to her plate. "I guarantee you won't be disappointed."

They were mostly silent while they ate, keeping to short and simple topics—the weather, the piped-in music, whether or not they would have leftovers.

As the server cleared away their empty dishes roughly half an hour later, headlights swept across the wall of windows at the front of the building. Then Brenna's phone vibrated against the table.

She tapped the screen and sighed before flicking her thumbs back and forth. "My dad's here. He wants to come in and get me, but I told him I was okay. He's way too overprotective, even more so now than he used to be."

Christy searched the front pocket of her wallet after she returned her credit card to its slot. "Here's my business card with my cell number and email. I'm in between jobs right now because of a move, but I'll see if I can connect with a local home-health service or doctor's office so we can make sure everything is on the up and up. I'll start putting out feelers Monday morning."

"I'm really glad you stopped. Thank you for that. And everything." Brenna tucked the card in her purse and slipped her arms into her coat sleeves. "I'll call you tomorrow."

CHAPTER TWO

"Dad, it's fine." His daughter's eye-roll as she picked up her coffee mug reminded Sven Carlsen of her teenage years. "Really. I'm an adult and I'd like to be treated like one."

She was right, but damned if he didn't want to bundle her up and keep her safe like he had when she was a baby.

He poked at his eggs and tried for a more diplomatic approach. "I just wondered who you were with. We haven't gone out to eat since...you know, and—"

"You're allowed to say it. The car accident." Brenna leveled a frown at him. "Repeat after me. *The car accident.* I'm not going to freak out if you call it what it was."

His insides scrambled worse than his breakfast. That day, the call, the waiting to know the extent of her injuries—it had been the worst experience of his life.

He swallowed past the hard lump in his throat. "The... car...accident."

His voice cracked over the words, much like his heart had cracked open when he hadn't known if his little girl would live or die. He would've traded places with her in an instant.

The soft brush of her fingertips on his clenched fist brought him back from the cliff. "It wasn't anyone's fault, especially not yours. Shit happens sometimes, and you can't protect me from everything. Well, you could, but not being able to do anything would drive me bananas. Life is for living. That's the mantra of my support group."

Instead of gathering her in his arms and never letting her go, he wrapped his much bigger hand around hers and gave it a gentle squeeze. "I know. I'm just having a tough time accepting that you're all grown up and you want to live on your own again, especially when I can make all the adjustments you need. I like having you here and taking care of you."

"I know, and I love you for it." She pulled her hand away and fiddled with the remains of her toast. "If it'll make you feel better, I met this very kind woman when I was on my way home from the basketball game. And before you say anything, I'm not mad about my friends wanting to sit up in the bleachers where they could see the game. They offered to stay on the floor with me. I wasn't super comfortable about being there with so many people anyway, so I said I just wanted to say hi and that you were waiting for me outside. It was easier, and that's what felt best at the moment."

He fought a grunt and lost. Her so-called friends should've seen how uncomfortable she was. "So, who was this lady you met?"

She cradled her nearly empty mug in her palms and sipped her doctored coffee. "One of my wheels dropped into a hole when I was crossing the street and she stopped to help me. She was waiting at the light and, like, actually parked her car in the middle of the road, turned on the flashers, and got out. She didn't feel sorry for me, unlike most people who think they're being helpful, and she showed me how to get unstuck. Then she invited me to Lorenzo's for pizza. God, she taught me more about how to navigate an unaccommodating world in less than an hour than I learned in a month with the guy who left me high and dry. She's an occupational therapist and is in town for the holidays. Until sometime in January. Maybe longer. I'm going to call her this afternoon about scheduling some sessions. See? I'm being proactive."

"Is she licensed? We'll... You'll need to find out what—"

"Dad. You're doing it again." Setting down her mug, Brenna sighed. "It's already handled. She's in the process of moving, so she isn't working right now, but she's going to check into a temporary position with the same clinic my last OT worked for. She mentioned a couple other options too. I like her a lot, and I'm hoping I can convince her to stay for a while."

Although the woman would have to prove herself to him, Sven gave his daughter the benefit of the doubt. She was smart and independent, and he had no right to hold her back, even if it ate at his soul to adopt a hands-off approach to her care. "Okay. Do you need anything before I head over to Grandma and Grandpa's to fix the flashing around the chimney?"

"Nope." She rolled back from the table with her breakfast dishes in her lap. "I have a work project due next week, so I'm just hanging out in your office this morning."

"It's your office too, for as long as you want it." Yes, his comment probably rubbed her the wrong way, but he hated the thought of her living by herself again.

Cut the bullshit. You're the one who doesn't like living alone.

She opened the dishwasher and strained to reach the faucet to rinse her plate.

Resisting the urge to turn on the water took planting his

work boots on the floor, pressing his ass to his seat, and focusing on not gripping his own dish hard enough to break it. His jaw ached and his ears rang by the time the clink of her mug, fork, and plate told him she'd finished her task at the dishwasher.

Brenna wheeled to the table and picked up her mug. "I can't wait to have an accessible kitchen. Do you think the fundraiser will make enough money for the renovations to a house or apartment?"

Despite his feelings about her moving out again, he nodded. "I'll make it happen if that's what you want. Even if I have to dress up as Santa Claus myself."

"Oh, that reminds me. Mrs. Barber emailed me this morning. Her brother had to have emergency gall bladder surgery last night, so he isn't available this year. Should I tell her you're willing to fill in?"

He gave a curt nod, even though the thought of wearing a red suit and socializing was near the top of the list of things he'd rather not do. "For you? Yes. But there better be a rule against adults sitting on my lap."

"If you had a girlfriend, they might back off."

A shudder rippled through him. "I don't want or need a girlfriend."

Laughter echoed through the kitchen as his daughter left him to finish cleaning up.

The single women of Creekside had finally decided to leave him the hell alone since that horrible day eleven months ago. Even a few married ones had propositioned him over the years. If he'd been looking to get laid or married, he would've been in heaven. Unfortunately, he preferred the company of his hand to another soul-shattering breakup or an accidental pregnancy with his rebound mistake.

Been there. Done those. Never again.

He didn't regret being a father, but it hadn't worked out quite the way he'd hoped. His first and only love was to blame for that.

Maybe not entirely, but I didn't have a choice.

With a final wipe of the counter, he pushed that counter-productive memory from his mind. Life sometimes sucked. Besides, his daughter deserved all his affection.

He snagged his coat from the hook in the hall and poked his head into the room he'd transformed into a shared office on his way to the garage door. "I'll be back by lunchtime. Call or text if you need anything."

Brenna looked up from an open file on the desk. "Okay. Be careful up on the housetop, Santa."

"Always." A smile came easily for the most important person in his world. "Love you, Bee."

"Love you too, Dad." She blew him a kiss and grinned. "Mrs. Barber said she'll stop by Grandma and Grandpa's to drop off the Santa suit and a thank-you batch of buckeyes about ten thirty when she goes to have her hair done."

Smothering a groan, he dug his keys from his jeans pocket. "No adults. If you didn't make that clear, I will. See you in a few hours."

She snickered and set her fingers back on the keyboard. "I told her. She thinks we'll raise more money if you set aside at least half an hour for the single ladies to share their Christmas wishes with you, but it's up to you."

"Then the answer is no. I'm not letting anybody pimp me out for a few hundred bucks I can donate myself. I'm going now." He waved with his empty hand and stalked to the garage, slowing only to lock the door and shaking his head the whole way. "I'll donate all the damn materials and labor myself before I let a bunch of women hoping for a husband or a roll in the sack turn that fundraiser into a three-ring circus."

As soon as he backed out of the driveway, the gray clouds skidding across the sky decided to spit a mix of sleet and wet snowflakes at his windshield, adding to his grouchy mood. It showed no sign of stopping or changing to all snow during the four-block drive to his parents' house or the ten minutes unloading his extension ladder and supplies took. Fortunately, he'd done more difficult jobs in worse conditions.

At the start of his ascent to the roof, his mom appeared on the other side of the living room window. Her broad grin warned him she planned to ambush him with another fix-up attempt or a dinner invitation with a surprise guest.

He returned her wave and continued upward. "I need a woman in my life like I need to fall through a roof."

Focusing on the job at hand required enough concentration to wipe all thoughts of dating from his mind, especially with the weather making a safety harness necessary. No way would he risk an injury, not if it might keep him from being there for his daughter. She'd been his whole world since the day she was born, and nothing would ever change that.

He finally gathered the leftover supplies and then stepped back to inspect his handiwork an hour and a half later. The new materials sealed the area around the bricks a lot better than the patch job he'd done during the early days of Brenna's lengthy hospital stay. Hell, he'd barely managed to function for weeks after the accident.

Months, more like it.

With the unfastened rope looped over his shoulder and the box tucked under his arm, he swung his foot to the closest rung on the ladder to climb down. Sleet and wet snow became light drizzle as he reached the ground and freed himself from the harness. Then the sweep of headlights across the house from behind drew his attention to the driveway.

The front door opened as Mrs. Barber shut off the engine of her prized 1996 Lincoln Town Car. She'd been driving that boat a mile to the beauty salon and back home every four weeks since her husband had passed away right after he bought it for her. The decades-old vehicle probably had less than ten thousand miles, even with her weekly visit to the grocery store.

His mom unfurled the huge golf umbrella in her hand. "Wait for me, Janice!"

"Take your time, Mom. It might be slippery." He stowed the box in his truck and still beat his mother to the visitor's car. Then he held out his arm to the white-haired woman who had been not only his middle school English teacher but the town's favorite Mrs. Claus for a good many years as well. "I'll come back for the suit."

"Thank you for the offer, but I'm just as capable of walking as you are. You can carry the Santa suit. And don't forget the buckeyes!" Mrs. Barber pointed to the cookie tin on the passenger seat as she shifted her boot-clad feet to the slick driveway. Waving away his arm, she stood and ducked under the umbrella his mom carried. "Who ordered this nasty weather? It wasn't you, was it, Sven?"

His mother raised her eyebrows at him, her mind clearly going straight to her frequent observation—that he walked around like a storm cloud more often than not.

Ignoring her insinuation, he stalked to the other side for the garment bag laying on the backseat and the tin in the front. "Why would I do that when I had to go up on the roof this morning? Head inside. I'll be right behind you after I put these in the truck."

His former teacher leaned in toward his mom, who glanced his direction over her shoulder with a troublemaking grin spreading across her face. The co-conspirators clearly had something up their sleeves and, without a doubt, it involved butting into his personal life.

He caught up with them in the kitchen, but he kept his mouth shut. Commenting would only bring more suffering down on him.

With the cupboard door open, his mom looked over her shoulder at him. "Want to warm up with a cup of something? Janice and I are having tea, but there's still some of your father's paint thinner from breakfast."

A bark of laughter echoed through the space, far outsizing the five-foot-nothing octogenarian it came from. "I remember when my Harold drank coffee so strong it could strip the varnish off a wood floor. It's a wonder he had any insides left."

Shaking his head, he held out his hand for a mug. "What doesn't kill you makes you stronger."

"Speaking of killing, it wouldn't hurt you to—"

"No grown women are sitting on this Santa's lap." He poured an inch of dark brew into his cup and inhaled the wonderfully bitter scent of aged coffee. It matched his feelings toward most women perfectly. "I'm not in the market for a girlfriend, wife, date, hookup, or even a housekeeper."

The stubborn set of Mrs. Barber's shoulders made his stomach knot. "But we could raise so much—"

"I don't care. The women of this town can go apply for a job at the strip club up the highway if they want to give somebody a lap dance." A huge gulp of his dad's brown sludge fortified his mood. "That's my final decision. If it isn't acceptable, find yourself another Santa Claus."

Despite her grimace, his former teacher gave a curt nod. "Suit yourself. I'll see you Saturday morning at nine thirty in the high school's main hall. You can put on the suit in the nurse's office."

"Okay." Not giving her a chance to change her mind, he rinsed his mug and headed for the front door. "Thank you for the buckeyes, Mrs. Barber. Mom, tell Dad the flashing's fixed. You shouldn't have any more problems with it."

Whispers followed him down the hall and finally ended when he stepped outside and shut the door.

No amount of conspiring would convince him to change his mind about women and dating.

CHAPTER THREE

CHRISTY FIDDLED WITH THE SHEAF OF PAPERS THE LAWYER had given her on Saturday morning and hoped the conversation with her potential client sidetracked her thoughts from the contents of the legal documents. "Tell me about yourself."

"I graduated from college two and a half years ago with a degree in architecture, got a full-time job where I did my internship, lived in my own apartment, paid my own bills. Eleven months ago, a man's brain aneurysm ruptured as he was driving home from work. His SUV hit my car when he ran a red light. I woke up in the hospital three weeks later with a spinal cord injury and no feeling from my waist down." Despite Brenna's succinct description, the sudden change in her voice told Christy the trauma still, not unexpectedly, lived on in the young woman's mind. "The only reason I know what happened is because there were eyewitness accounts and his wife came to visit me three or four times a week while I was hospitalized. Her husband died at the scene, leaving her and their two teenage kids behind. He was only forty years old."

Smothering her reaction took much less effort over the

phone than it would have in person. It didn't, however, prevent a surge of grief—for all the victims of that horrible tragedy.

"It's actually fairly common to never fully regain those memories." She forced herself to direct the discussion away from that aspect, knowing from experience and training that sympathy instead of empathy would only prolong Brenna's tendency to define herself by the accident and her inability to walk instead of who she was. "I've never met an architect before. Tell me more about it. What kind of buildings do you design?"

Her redirection seemed to work when Brenna launched into an enthusiastic description of past and current projects. After several minutes of chatting about a career she obviously enjoyed, the young woman laughed. "Sorry. I can get a little carried away, talking about all the fun stuff I get to do. I'm lucky to have a great boss. She held my job for me while I was recovering and offered to let me work remotely as long as I get the job done."

"No need to apologize. You love what you do, which is more that a lot of people can say. I'm really glad to hear your boss has allowed that flexibility." Christy straightened the will, stuffed it back in its envelope, and slid it into her computer bag. Out of sight might not guarantee out of mind, but it certainly wouldn't hurt. "I never sleep well in hotels, so I did a little research on the occupational therapy prac-tices in the area last night. Some names were familiar. People I've met at conferences, worked with at one time or another, a few from college. Since I already have connec-tions with them, I sent several emails to see if they know of any openings or temporary positions. I'm planning to contact a few more places after our phone call. In the mean-time, tell me what your goals are. What you'd like to accomplish. Where you see yourself a few months or a year from now."

"Hmm." At least ten seconds of silence passed, hinting that Brenna was hesitant about sharing her thoughts. As determined as she'd been to get home by herself from the basketball game last night, she had to have some wishes and dreams for the future.

"What's the most important thing you want to achieve? No wrong answers, and I promise not to laugh or try to convince you to think smaller."

"I, uh…" A noisy exhale carried through the phone. "I want to live on my own again. Either a small single-story house or a first-floor apartment with a ramp and wide hallways. Lower kitchen and bathroom counters. Everything made to work with my disability, without inconveniencing my dad in his house because he thinks he should take care of me now. I know he means well, but I'm a grownup, and I want to be treated like one. The city council voted to use this year's annual fundraiser to help pay for renovations. You probably saw signs for it when you drove through town. Claus for a Cause. It's next weekend. I'd like to use the money to make the necessary changes on my own place."

"This is what I'm talking about." A surge of pride chased away the lingering ache for all Brenna had lost.

"The only problem is finding someplace in town. The few apartment options here are mostly older homes that have been split into duplexes—upstairs-downstairs spaces. Not that there are many available. And the real estate market here is practically nonexistent. People don't move in and out of Creekside very often."

As the manila envelope of legal documents caught Christy's eye a few inches away, an idea formed in her head. The solution to the stress-inducing situation of dealing with her father's estate was simple—if she could make it work the way she wanted to. She scribbled a note to email the lawyer with the numerous questions that immediately filled her thoughts. "So, this is a good start. Make a list and think about the steps to make those things happen. It should be like a resolution list, but you can make it any time, not just for the new year."

"Okay." Confidence and drive came through in Brenna's response, a sure sign she was prepared to work hard to succeed. "Oh no! This is bad. Really bad."

Alarm bells went off, setting Christy's nerve endings on edge. "What's wrong? Are you okay? Do you need me to call 9-1-1 or come over?"

"Sorry! I didn't mean to scare you. I'm good, but I got an email from Mrs. Barber that she needs to go stay with her very pregnant granddaughter for a few days. Her grandson-in-law has to travel for his job or something, and the baby is due any time now." Brenna groaned. "Crap. This completely messes up Mrs. Claus's Cookie Kitchen on Saturday. We've already assigned all the volunteers to their posts and our backup Mrs. C relocated to Columbus in September. You wouldn't happen to love making cookies, would you?"

The unstoppable urge to revert to doormat helper slammed into Christy, despite her decision to avoid inter-acting with the residents of her former hometown. She aimed a glare at the gallon bag of biscotti she'd made to get her through the ordeal of dredging up the past. Cookies had been her stress outlet for years—both making and eating them.

I already offered my OT services.

But... Okay, maybe I can do more to support Brenna without anyone being the wiser.

She forced the tension from her spine with a slow exhale. "Is there a costume? Like a wig and glasses?"

"Yeah, but if that's a deal-breaker, we can probably change things up a bit. You know, modernize the Mrs. to Ms. Claus and give her a dye job and a stylish pantsuit or something." Brenna sounded awfully desperate for a replacement. "You don't have to do the baking part, either. You'll help decorate cookies in the Family and Consumer Sciences lab with anybody who wants to participate. Frost a cookie. Add sprinkles. That kind of thing. Send them off to the next stop when they're done. You just have to supervise, restock the decorating supplies on the tables, and talk to the kids."

Surrendering to her penchant for coming to the rescue, Christy hoped she didn't regret being part of the big community event. "Actually, I don't mind wearing Mrs. Barber's costume, assuming it fits."

"That's awesome! Thanks so much. Really." Clicking and clacking in the background suggested the young woman was typing an email to the original Mrs. Claus. "I've let Mrs. Barber know I found her replacement and that she'll need to drop off the costume to one of us."

No backing out now.

"Oh, I should also mention you'll hang out with Santa for a few hours after the cookie kitchen closes. The kids can sit on his lap if they want to. You hand out the goodie bags and then pose with them for pictures. It's up to you if you want to join everybody for the chili supper in the cafeteria. You get to eat for free since you're a volunteer, but you might be ready for a break, so don't feel obligated. Caroling in the park is at seven, with hot chocolate and cider booths. Again, not mandatory."

Brenna's excitement muffled Christy's mixed emotions. The festival had grown significantly in the twenty-seven years since she'd left Creekside—and had changed to a fundraising opportunity for residents in need of assistance.

Not once in her childhood had she attended the annual event. The one time she'd asked, her father had shipped her off to her grandparents' for the holidays early, before winter break even started.

She closed her eyes and took a deep breath to calm the unease that had settled in with the news of his death.

I can do this. It'll help me find closure.

The tightness in her muscles slowly eased, allowing her to focus on the present. She opened the calendar on her laptop. "If you have a list of where I need to be at what time, would you mind emailing me a copy? And you said Saturday, right?"

"Yep, all day Saturday. I'm sending the itinerary with notes about times and places now. There. Done. Let me know if you don't get it in the next ten minutes and I'll resend."

"Great. Thanks." A notification popped up on the screen, so she navigated to her email account. "It's h— I thought I got it, but it's a response from one of the people I contacted last night. Okay, here's your email. Do you have time to hold on while I see what my former classmate has to say?"

"Sure. Fingers crossed."

A second response appeared as Christy moved the cursor to the first, sparking a combination of hope and apprehension. Bad news usually traveled faster than good news, didn't it?

She opened the email from the guy who'd lived down the hall in her apartment building during her final year of grad school. After a cheery paragraph with news about his wife and two children, he raved over her perfect timing. His office had been shorthanded for several months, and her experience meant he was willing to go to bat with his partners to hire her on the spot in whatever capacity she was willing to accept.

Her doubts cleared, but she moved on to the next reply. Again, a job offer practically jumped off the page, this time for a permanent position if she could be convinced by the salary. When she returned to her inbox, a third and a fourth had been delivered.

She took a quick look at both before swallowing the lump of emotion in her throat. Having choices wasn't something she'd ever expected or encountered. "I have four emails so far. We can pick whichever location is most convenient for you. Or if you prefer a certain provider over another, we can go that route."

"That's amazing news. I knew you were good at your job, but this is… Wow. Your peers must really respect you. How soon can we start?"

Brenna's observation gave Christy a boost of confidence she hadn't known she needed. Being back where she'd grown up brought up more feelings than she wanted to deal with. "I have some things I have to do this morning. Are you free for lunch? We can discuss the details of each option and make the decision together."

"Lunch sounds great, but it's my turn to pay this time. How about Maxwell's Diner on High Street at twelve thirty? I haven't had their grilled cheese in forever."

Thrilled for her new friend's willingness to try another outing after the trouble on Friday, Christy shoved aside her own reluctance to venture to an old haunt. "Sounds terrific. I love grilled cheese. Meet you out front."

"Perfect. See you in a few hours."

Several minutes of silence passed before she finally slipped her phone into her purse and withdrew her car keys. Delaying the first trip to her childhood home since she'd left Creekside wouldn't make it any easier.

Her stomach adamantly disagreed during the entire six-block drive and when she parked in front of the single-car garage that housed her father's old work van. Instead of letting the past take over, she forced herself to walk to the porch, unlock the front door, and enter the modest house that held too many memories.

His ancient recliner sat in the same corner, facing a newer-looking TV. The couch where she'd done her homework all through school still stretched along the wall between the living room and the kitchen. Even the bookshelf that held her worn copies of *Little Women*, *Black Beauty*, and numerous other favorites hadn't changed or been moved from its place next to the coat closet. A light layer of dust dulled every surface, but clutter was nonexistent and the space said nothing about him or the way he'd lived since her departure.

A pang of regret tried to fight through the numbness, but she buried it with the other feelings she'd long ago relegated to the past. He'd chosen to lie to her about her mother, letting her believe she'd been the cause of her mother's death. Childbirth hadn't taken that woman away from them. Her mother had chosen to leave, and he'd chosen to hide the truth to protect his pride.

Christy plodded down the hall toward the bedrooms, half hoping they were uninhabitable and would necessitate staying at the hotel rather than living temporarily in a space with ghosts from her previous life. The expense might punish her bank account, but that was better than facing her already battered emotions for days and nights on end.

She stopped at the closed door to her bedroom. Her heart hammered in her chest as she reached for the knob with a shaking hand.

Just do it and get it over with.

The door swung inward, revealing what amounted to an abandoned tomb. Her hastily made bed, the books piled on her nightstand, a partially open dresser drawer—all of it suggested she'd left yesterday instead of nearly thirty years ago. The only hints she'd been gone longer were a thick coating of dust everywhere and cobwebs fluttering where the ceiling met the walls. Not a fingerprint or footstep marred the surfaces. Clearly, no one had entered her room since her hasty departure.

Did he even miss me?

She shuffled to her father's room at the end of the hall. Since he could no longer give her a stern warning to stay out, she crossed the threshold for a closer inspection. It was every bit as sparsely decorated as it had been when she'd lived with him, but the floor looked like it had been swept recently— possibly a day or two prior to his trip to the hospital to die— and the furniture and bedding looked relatively clean.

I can do this.

A quick search of the broom closet in the kitchen yielded a sweeper and the cleaning supplies she needed to prepare the master bedroom for her temporary habitation. How much would he hate her invasion of his privacy?

Considering all the times he'd shut down her questions, he was probably rolling over in his grave and thinking about haunting her—as if she didn't have enough ghosts escaping from the excess baggage she carried with her everywhere.

Two and a half hours flew by while she washed the bedding, swept and dusted all but her old room, and remade the bed. She would have to tackle the closet, dresser, night-stand, and scuffed wooden desk at some point, but the thought of sorting through his private things made her stomach roil. Besides, she had a lunch appointment with her soon-to-be client.

The brisk walk brought back more memories—some good, some bad.

Brenna wheeled toward her as she approached Maxwell's, a fixture in Creekside since well before she was born. The young woman's cheery expression chased away the cold seeping through Christy's leggings.

Pulling open the door, Christy shook off the depressing mood being in her childhood home had sparked and returned her lunch date's smile. "Hi. I've been looking forward to figuring out our plan since we talked this morning."

With less effort than entering the pizza place had required, Brenna rolled into the diner. "Me too. I even managed the half-mile trip without getting permanently stuck in a pothole."

"That's awesome. You're a quick learner." With a gesture toward the PLEASE WAIT TO BE SEATED sign, Christy let her companion take the lead.

Brenna glanced up at her before waving at the apron-clad woman hurrying toward them. "Hi, Mrs. Ferris."

The server's eyes widened. "Oh my goodness, as I live and breathe. Brenna, it's so good to see you out and about. What can I do for you, honey?"

"It's good to see you too." After a barely noticeable pause, her lunch date nodded toward the dining room. "Table for two please. If it's not too much trouble, can we have the empty table in the far corner?"

"Of course." The server grabbed a pair of menus from the greeter's stand. "Follow me."

Without any prompting, their guide slid a chair to the back wall and then took their drink order. "I'll get those hot chocolates while you look over today's specials."

As soon as their lunch was delivered, Christy opened the list she'd made on her phone so they could narrow down the choices. "Before we really dive in, type in your full name and contact information in my notes to pass on to whichever facility we decide to go with. It should speed up the process a little."

Brenna's fingers danced over the screen for less than a minute and she handed back Christy's cell. "Let me know if you need anything else."

She nodded as she read what the young woman had typed. *Brenna Carlsen.*

Her heart stuttered at the sight of her new client's last name. The young woman's bright blue eyes matched Sven's.

Had she really expected her high school boyfriend to remain single forever? To not marry and have children? To not move on?

CHAPTER FOUR

"Let me see."

"Just a sec." Sven grimaced at his reflection in the mirror before he stalked to the bedroom door to open it for his daughter. "I look ridiculous. The sleeves are too short and the hat is too small."

"Are you saying you have orangutan arms and a fat head?" Brenna grinned up at him, clearly amused by her teasing and his discomfort. Tugging on the front of the suit jacket, she pulled him closer and turned up the cuff of one sleeve. "No worries. See? It has buttons to adjust the length. Same with the hat. Hand it over and I'll fix it."

"So much for getting out of playing Santa." At her immediate frown, he sighed and followed her instructions. "I'm kidding. I'll do whatever it takes to make sure the fundraiser goes well. Do you think I need more stuffing?"

She poked a finger into the pillow he'd strapped on under the red coat. "Nope. You'll split the seams if we add another layer. I want to see the beard, and put the hat back on with it."

"Have you always been this bossy?" Despite an effort not to smile, part of one slipped out as he picked up the pile of cottony fluff from the dresser. Her self-confidence and take-charge personality had always made him proud to be her father.

Her laughter echoed off the walls. "You know it."

Fifteen minutes and a nod of approval later, he rehung the costume in his closet and laced up his hiking boots. The roofing business slowed considerably during the colder months, but estimates, ice dams, the occasional repair, and an inspection here and there kept him from being bored from December to March. Thankfully, he wasn't stuck inside doing accounts receivable today.

As he pocketed his cell phone, it buzzed in his hand. A quick check revealed a new addition to his and Brenna's shared calendar. He stepped into their office to let her know he'd seen it. "That was fast. Did your new therapist get connected with an office already?"

She nodded without glancing his direction. Her eyebrows scrunched downward as she seemed to concentrate on the computer monitor almost blocking his view of her. "She had eight job offers by the end of our lunch meeting on Monday, so you have no reason whatsoever to question her qualifications. We discussed the options and picked one together because she wanted to be sure I was comfortable with the choice and that the location wouldn't be a problem. She filled out her employment paperwork yesterday morning, so we're all set. The office just confirmed my first appointment for Friday at two."

Her reassurance about the therapist's experience and actually having a job eased some of his concerns. "It's supposed to snow on Friday. I have an estimate scheduled at one thirty, but I'll switch it to earlier in the day so I can drive you there."

"You don't need to do that. Just drop me off on your way. The office is a few doors down from the library and I got a notification that a book I've been wanting to read is available."

That she didn't insist on getting there on her own was a win, so he gave a curt nod. "That works. I need to head out, but I'll be back in time to make supper. Spaghetti or fajitas?"

"Oh, fajitas!" She finally looked over at him and grinned. "I'll make the guacamole."

Seeing her happy made his heart swell. "Sounds good. See you later. Love you, Bee."

"Love you too, Dad." She blew a kiss at him, like she had every day when he'd watched her walk into preschool and elementary school from the drop-off lane.

He fought to swallow past the lump in his throat as he stalked to the garage. How the hell had his little girl grown up so fast?

For a fair part of that time, they had lived with his parents. He'd relied on his mom and dad for babysitting services and so much more during the earliest years. Their support had gotten him through being a single dad while his daughter grew into the amazing young woman she was now —and they still propped him up on a regular basis.

She should have been mine and—

He blocked that automatic thought from his mind.

Should've, would've, could've didn't change the past and wouldn't bring back the girl he'd loved, no matter how often his stupid heart wished for it.

He buckled up while he waited for the garage door to rise behind him, fighting the same battle he'd waged against his feelings for more years than he dared admit to.

Autopilot kicked in as he drove toward his first appointment of the day. He'd walked, ridden, and driven the route to and past her house hundreds or maybe thousands of times in his life. Most days he was able to resist looking, but something inside urged him to take a last glimpse of the now-unin-habited Craftsman home since her father had passed away two weeks ago. In a perfect world, it would have a FOR SALE sign in the front yard, killing any lingering hope that she might return. The hope that refused to budge reignited as soon as the mailbox came into view.

Enough already.

He couldn't keep doing this, setting himself up for disap-pointment day after day.

She'd sworn she wasn't coming back, and her promise had held true. That fact wasn't going to change.

His gut twisted at the sight of a car parked in the drive-way. A heartbeat later, a figure appeared on the porch with a bulging garbage bag in tow. It was nearly half the person's size. A brown ponytail the same shade as his first-and-only love's hung partway down her back.

Then she turned toward the street, revealing dark eyes and a serious mouth he would know anywhere. He'd kissed those lips for the first time when he was fourteen and the last time on the day before she'd left Creekside at eighteen.

She looked up, like she knew he was there. A momentary visual connection sent an electric shock zipping through his body, short-circuiting every part of him, but he jerked his gaze away and kept driving. If she'd wanted anything to do with him, she would've searched him out, not that he was hard to find. She hadn't made even a minimal effort.

His chest tightened and didn't loosen at all through an inspection in the town ten miles up the road and an estimate for a barn roof replacement a few miles closer. Life went on, with or without his participation or approval, but seeing her seriously tempted him to ask for a second chance. How could his soul ache so damn much after nearly three decades?

He continued going through the motions for the rest of the

afternoon until he detoured around her block on his way home. Avoidance could never purge her from his heart, soul, or brain, but at least the odds of seeing her again were considerably lower.

Despite the lingering pain, he made the final turn onto his street and let out a slow exhale. Brenna had always picked up on extra stress he carried with him and ferreted out what was bothering him. This baggage needed to stay locked in a closet well out of her reach.

He pressed the garage-door opener button and took another deep breath to calm his wound-up nerves. Before he pulled into the space that had once held his truck and Brenna's car, the kitchen entrance swung wide and she rolled forward. Her wide smile chased away most of the sickening feelings still churning in his stomach.

She waved her arms, like she wanted him to hurry, so he grabbed his lunchbox and exited the cab of his truck. "What's up? Did you find somebody else to dress up as Santa?"

Her grin became an all-out laugh as she backed up to let him in the house. "Nope, because I'm not looking. You're never going to believe what happened today! It's a hundred times better. Seriously, a thousand or a million."

He tempered the first thought that popped into his head— that she'd regained some sensation in her legs or feet. The doctors had told him an expectation of that magnitude wasn't within the realm of possibilities. He closed the door behind him and set his lunchbox on the counter. "Give me a second to take off my coat and sit down."

"I can't wait! But you're definitely going to want to sit for this news." She tugged on his sleeve and gestured to the closest chair. As soon as his ass landed on the seat, she handed him a manila envelope. "So, you know how I said my new therapist is in town for the holidays? A relative left a house to her in the will, and she offered to sell it to me. For a *dollar*. She isn't planning to stay here and she knows I've been trying to find an apartment or something to make accessible. She's practically *giving* it to me. How cool is that? We can look at it before I decide, but she thinks it can be renovated to work with my chair. Her lawyer will handle all the paperwork. The envelope has a detailed description of the property, a copy of the survey, and an appraisal. Do you have an hour or two to go see it tomorrow?"

Your own house? Not yet.

Ignoring the guilty twinge in his gut, he nodded. "Morning is better, but I'll rearrange my schedule if I have to. Make the appointment and we'll look at it."

The hopeful tears in her eyes as she held out her arms tightened the knot in his stomach. "Thank you, Dad. You're the best."

He gathered her into a careful hug that lasted until she fake-coughed, like he was smothering her. After a quick kiss on her forehead, he loosened his hold. "Anything for you, Bee."

"I'm so lucky you're my dad." She gave him another squeeze. "I'll text Christy right now."

"Christy?" The word came out more breath than sound.

"Christy Rime. Didn't I tell you her name already? I thought I did, but maybe not." With her phone in her palm, Brenna tapped at the screen. "She's usually really quick to reply, so we should have a time set up before supper. Do you need me to chop anything?"

Christy Rime.

A million unbidden memories flitted through his mind, accompanied by too many feelings to process.

What had his daughter said?

She isn't staying in Creekside.

The prospect of seeing his former love and having to watch her leave again reopened the old wounds that had never fully healed. He had numbed himself to a certain extent, but he'd given up on ever truly moving beyond the pervasive heartache that wouldn't fade.

Blindsided by seeing her and discovering she was part of his daughter's recovery, he sat in silence for several minutes, waiting to wake up from whatever hellish dream this was.

"Dad. Dad?" Brenna frowned at him. "Are you feeling okay? You didn't fall today, did you?"

"Of course not." His response came out gruffer than he intended, and forcing a smile wasn't something he could do at the moment. "Did you make the guacamole?"

Her intense stare warned him she hadn't fallen for his attempt to change the subject. "Let's have spaghetti instead. What's wrong? Is this about me mov—"

The cell chirped in her lap, saving him from the question he had no desire to answer.

She flipped it over and swiped upward. "She wants to know if we can come over now. I'm telling her we'll be there in ten minutes."

A wave of nausea and lightheadedness kept him in the chair when he would've preferred escaping to a rooftop. He shoved his fingers through his hair and grunted.

Her sigh reminded him of her teenage years. "I know you don't want me to move out, but I'm ready to be on my own again. Besides, it's only like three blocks away. She sent me the address."

Two blocks. Less than half a mile.

He could walk there in his sleep.

"You're not mad, are you?"

At her softly spoken question, he shook his head. "I've never been mad at you. Ever. Not once in your entire life.

Grab your coat. It'll take a few minutes to get you and your chair loaded in the truck."

"Okay." Without another word, she rolled out of the room, navigating the corner into the hallway like a pro.

Nine minutes later, he parked behind the same car he'd seen this morning and shut down the emotions trying to crawl through his skin. Brenna deserved to be happy, even if it was at his own expense, and he sure as hell wasn't about to let Christy see how affected he was by her temporary return.

Giving my daughter a house doesn't make up for leaving me in your dust.

He buried the jumble of grief, anger, and hurt deeper than before while he unloaded the wheelchair from the covered bed and helped Brenna into the seat. Then he followed her to a ramp leading to the front door.

It swung inward at their approach, revealing an older but no less beautiful version of his former best friend turned longtime girlfriend. Her gaze darted away from his and landed in the vicinity of his daughter. "Sorry for the short notice. My new boss wants me to run a training session at the clinic tomorrow."

So that's the way you're going to play it?

"No worries. My dad just got home from work right before you texted, and I was done for the day." Brenna looked up at him. "Dad, this is Christy Rime. Christy, meet my dad. Sven Carlsen."

His lungs stalled when his lost love slowly extended her right hand past the handle at the back of the wheelchair. Then she locked familiar brown eyes on his, but the bare hint of a smile was framed by a tense jaw. "Mr. Carlsen."

He swallowed to wet his suddenly parched throat as he battled a snarky greeting sure to pique Brenna's curiosity. If

Christy wanted to pretend they were strangers, he could too. "Ms. Rime."

The first touch of her fingers sent a jolt up his arm and zinging straight to his groin. Her eyes widened, suggesting she'd felt it too.

It doesn't mean a damn thing. She's leaving in January. She'll always leave.

He stuffed his still-tingling fist in his coat pocket. "Let's take a tour."

She led them to the living room with the same couch from their days doing homework together. Her father's chair filled the same corner it had back then. The hardwood floor could use a light sanding and a coat of varnish, and the walls needed a fresh coat of paint. Otherwise, the room seemed to be in decent shape—basically unchanged since his last visit.

The rest of the interior passed his visual inspection. The kitchen and bathroom might require some plumbing and electrical updates during the accessibility renovation, but Brenna had no problem fitting her chair through the few doorways and the short hall. He had to admit it had a lot of potential, even with reminders of the past seeping out of every wall.

Leaving his daughter and her therapist inside, he walked the perimeter to note any exterior issues on his phone. The dilapidated bench in the backyard tempted him to wade through summers of digging in the dirt and winters of building snow forts, but he shook off the impulse to recall memories that included their first kiss under the maple tree.

She wasn't staying, and he needed to remember that.

He added a last note to climb on the roof during daylight hours and then stalked to the front of the house, determined not to fall into her trap again.

Brenna waited beside Christy at the bottom of the ramp. "What do you think, Dad?"

Keeping his attention on his phone, he grunted. "I have some questions and I'd like a structural engineer to look at it."

"Okay." His daughter turned toward the bane of his existence. "I bet you know some of the answers, Christy. Why don't you come have supper with us?"

His insides nearly revolted at the thought of spending another second with her, let alone a whole meal.

Is a twenty-four-year-old too old for a grounding?

CHAPTER FIVE

CHRISTY PUSHED AWAY THE REMAINS OF HER PARTIALLY EATEN lunch, leaned her elbows on her desk, and cradled her head as she closed her eyes. She'd barely slept the last two nights, ever since trying to prove the past had no hold over her. Clearly, it did, despite married men being off-limits. That was only one of the reasons she'd lied to Brenna about having a prior commitment so she wouldn't have to join them for supper and meet Sven's wife.

One touch of his skin against hers with a simple hand-shake had lain to rest the ridiculous notion that she was over him. He obviously hadn't had any issues moving on with his life, although a grudge seemed to be set firmly in place where she was concerned.

The sweet boy she'd grown up with no longer had an easy smile for her or readable expressions—unless stoic and unap-proachable counted. Only when he spoke to his daughter did his face soften.

Unlike my father.

His lips had always thinned and his frown lines had deep-ened when she was present. She hadn't understood why until she'd accidently found a woman's picture and a Dear John letter relinquishing her parental rights to him for a baby girl with no name.

What a way to celebrate my eighteenth birthday.

He must've seen her mother every time he looked at her, but it didn't justify saying her mom had died during childbirth. He'd lied to her, blaming her for a death that hadn't occurred, even as he raised her with no hint of affection.

He punished me for what she did.

Nothing in his desk, dresser, or nightstand had contradicted his behavior toward her or hinted at any love on his part. Why had he even bothered to keep her? Had she been nothing more than a convenient catalyst for his bitterness?

That bitterness had carried over into her life, in spite of her efforts to remain positive and project happiness. She had survived being in her childhood home this week, but seeing Sven had brought the opposite of closure.

All the more reason to leave as soon as possible.

Though Brenna would likely be disappointed, Christy didn't belong here.

Her cell buzzed on her desk, alerting her to their afternoon session in thirty minutes. She mentally crossed her fingers that he didn't plan to stick around for the hour-long appointment. The tension might drive her mad, and his daughter didn't need an overprotective audience while she learned new skills and practiced old ones.

No motherly audience, either, while we're at it.

Christy tossed the rest of her lunch in the trash and carried her work laptop to the modified kitchen down the hall. Her normal routine included a review of her new patient's medical history. This time would be no different, in case something in the files hadn't come up in conversation.

Standing at the adjustable counter, she logged in and

clicked through to Brenna's records. The details of her injuries amplified Christy's admiration for the young woman who'd almost died. Her road to recovery over the last eleven months demonstrated her strength and a profound determination to not only live, but to excel in a world that presented challenges on a daily basis.

A brief vibration against her hip pulled Christy out of the pages and pages of documentation. Her phone showed a text message from her soon-to-arrive client.

"Goal #1: To not be a burden to my dad or my grandparents.

Goal #2: To live as independently as possible in my own house or apartment.

Goal #3: To learn all I can about how to advocate for myself and others with disabilities."

The amount of respect she had for Brenna grew tenfold. Most of the people she worked with started out small, like preparing a meal or going on an outing by themselves— which were terrific achievements soon after life-altering injuries and illnesses. Seldom did anyone aim high at the beginning of their journey, let alone for the long term.

She savored an unexpected rush of pride as she responded. *"I'm beyond impressed. Practically speechless. I have no doubt you'll accomplish all of them."*

A row of red hearts appeared a few seconds later. *"Aw, shucks. Will be there in five minutes. I was told I need to sign some forms."*

"See you soon." As Christy closed out of the records tab, something niggled at her. She couldn't pinpoint what it was, but she'd missed an important bit of information about the case. She had learned to trust that feeling as a child, and her intuition never failed her.

The cursor sat in the middle of the emergency contact

page, waiting for her to move the arrow, click on a different tab, or change data in the current form.

She absently read through the listed names, phone numbers, and relationship to the patient while her brain figured out what didn't add up in her mind.

Sven Carlsen. Father. Otto and Maggie Carlsen. Grandparents.

Mother. Why isn't her mother listed?

Was Sven widowed? Or had he suffered a contentious divorce?

Or she could have a job that doesn't make her a good choice for an emergency contact.

Her future with the boy she'd loved had perished the day Christy had saved herself, and no amount of yearning would bring it back to life.

"Here you go. Enjoy your first session." With a bright smile, the office manager motioned for Brenna to enter the room.

"Hi, Christy." Brenna wheeled her chair into the room past her escort, her coat and gloves on her lap. "I know I'm early, but I had a book to pick up at the library and my dad has a two-o'clock appointment. It was easier for him to drop me off than reschedule."

Relegating her pointless speculations to the part of her brain with a padlock, Christy waved the young woman forward. "No worries. I was just catching up on your medical history. Are you ready to get started?"

"Ready and willing." Using the more efficient arm motions they'd talked about when they met, Brenna crossed to the fully functional kitchen. "How does this work? Am I learning to use normal counters first?"

"Today we'll be practicing with standard-height counter-tops since you need some training until you have ADA-compliant counters." Christy pressed the down button on the control pad and released it when the main unit reached its lowest setting. "I'll also introduce you to the lower ones you'll have after your renovations are done."

"Wow! This is so cool." Staring toward the setup of a built-in stovetop, accessible sink, and a dozen other top-of-the-line features that raised and lowered, Brenna backed up, withdrew her cell from her purse, and snapped several pictures. "I need the name of the company where I can order the whole setup. I've missed cooking so much."

"Of course. I'll get the printout with information on this manufacturer and a few others while you hang up your coat and see what's in all the drawers and cabinets. Be right back." The trip to the front desk gave Christy time to shove her feelings about Sven and the past a little deeper into their locked box. She had a job to do—a job she loved.

The next two hours passed quickly as she guided Brenna through several methods to adapt and be proficient in a typical and a chair-friendly kitchen, as well as helping her practice wheelies. Nothing seemed to be too much of a challenge for her all-time favorite client.

Christy retrieved the vegetable and cheese trays and the batch of peanut butter no-bake cookies they'd prepared from the refrigerator and placed them in a bag. "Great job. What's your most useful takeaway from today's session?"

"Bigger isn't necessarily better." Brenna's wide grin and giggle-snort lit up her face. "I had a lot more leverage when I was cutting at the table than I did at the higher counter. Oh, and taste-testing is always allowed when making cookies."

The young woman's witty sense of humor drew a laugh from Christy. "And at least half of tonight's supper is ready."

"Actually, I was thinking… I'm in the mood for Mexican food, and there's this place on the other side of town that has amazing fajitas. Are you busy tonight?" Brenna looked up at her with a hopeful smile.

"I don't want to intrude if you and your family have plans." Fishing for information wasn't her style, but the words came out before Christy could control her mouth. She absolutely did not want to know the specifics of her former boyfriend's personal life. Interacting with him during the walk-through of her late father's house had already caused enough conflicting feelings and unwanted thoughts.

"You won't be intruding. I promise. It's just Dad and me. I don't have a mom or any brothers or sisters. Well, I have a biological mom, of course, but she and my dad weren't dating anymore when she found out she was pregnant. She planned to give me up for adoption, but he wanted me. So, long story short, she's not in the picture. Never has been, which is totally okay with me. One awesome parent is better than a hundred bad ones. Do you have any kids?"

Christy's vision wavered and she clutched the table to keep her balance. Brenna had one parent, like she had, but the similarities evidently ended there. Sven had willingly accepted his role as father and supported his daughter in every way.

Just Dad and me. Funny how that can be the best or the worst possible thing.

She sucked in a slow breath to steady the shifting floor and shook her head. "No. No husband. No kids."

I have no one.

"That's too bad. I bet you'd make a terrific mom." A chirp sounded, and Brenna flipped over the phone on her lap. "My ride's here. Please say you'll come. I'll text you the details."

"I..." Still feeling a little woozy, Christy sank into one of the chairs. "I'm not sure what's on my calendar."

Brenna's eye-roll sparked a guilt trip, because the excuse didn't fly with either of them.

"What if I need your advice on how to handle an accessibility issue?" Brenna maneuvered toward the corridor and glanced over her shoulder as she made the turn to head to the waiting room. "Thanks for the great session. See you at La Cocina at five thirty."

Resting her crossed arms on the table and her forehead on her arms, Christy closed her eyes and sighed. Sven immediately appeared behind her eyelids—not as an eighteen-year-old boy with a heart of gold, but as an impassive forty-five-year-old man who radiated keep-out vibes. He'd matured into a tall broad-shouldered grump with salt-and-pepper scruff that suited his guarded personality. Spending time with him would be a mistake, especially since she was leaving again soon.

But how can I say no to his daughter?

Brenna would continue to ask after every brush-off, of that she had no doubt.

Can I survive one awkward meal with him? Thank god, I'm busy all day tomorrow with the Claus for a Cause fundraiser.

Her phone hummed near her elbow, forcing her to make the decision.

A pleading-face emoji followed the name and address of the restaurant and the time. Someone almost certainly had a lot of experience wrapping people around her little finger.

"I'll see you then."

It was the only response that wouldn't result in massive self-reproach.

"Yay!!! I knew I'd wear you down eventually. Ha!"

A reluctant smile slipped free, warning Christy she had a major weakness where Brenna was concerned. Fortunately, no one and nothing could ever convince her to make Creek-side her home again.

She toted the laptop back to her office to type up her observations and recommendations, based on how the first therapy appointment had gone. The habit of noting a patient's starting point and progress distracted her from the past, the present, and what could've been until another text arrived.

"La Cocina is an 8-minute drive from the clinic and a 6-minute drive from your house with Friday traffic."

Despite the reindeer flying in circles in her stomach, she managed a chuckle at the messenger's persistence. As she shut down her computer, another message announced its arrival.

"Time to put your coat on—and your shoes, if you're at home and took them off."

This time she shook her head, but she did what she'd been told. She'd no sooner buttoned her wool coat than more instructions popped into the one-sided conversation.

"No time to go to the bathroom! There's a nice one where you're going. Grab your keys and purse and get in the car!"

A bark of laughter escaped, overtaking the case of nerves. Her dinner date evidently had no qualms about making things happen.

On her way to the parking lot, Christy tapped in a reply. *"I'm going. I'm going."*

"Good. See you in a few!"

Skirting Creekside's downtown, she arrived seven minutes later—right behind the pickup truck Sven and his daughter had driven to the house she'd inherited. She pulled into the closest empty space and used her rearview mirror to watch them park in an accessible spot near the entrance.

As Christy gathered her purse and adjusted her scarf, Sven retrieved Brenna's wheelchair from the covered bed, rolled it to the passenger side, and locked the wheels to keep it from moving. His care and gentleness as he transferred her into the chair backed up her earlier assertion that he was an awesome parent.

Christy trailed them into the restaurant with her heart in her throat. If her father had ever treated her with such kindness, she didn't remember it.

"Christy, you're here! You already met my dad, so you two can chat while I go see about getting a table." Brenna wasted no time excusing her way through the group of people in front of her.

Sven clenched his scruffy jaw, like he wanted to be anywhere other than here, and he didn't look away from the direction his daughter had gone. "Thanks for emailing Bee with the answers to my questions about the house."

She ignored his gruff tone since it seemed to be his default around her. "You're welcome."

"I'm working on lining up an engineer to checks things out too." His voice softened somewhat, but his face remained unreadable. "Is it okay if I come over and inspect the roof on Sunday?"

"Yes. Sure." Catching sight of Brenna waving them toward her, Christy stepped forward, glad for the inadvertent rescue. "Looks like our table is ready."

A grunt carried to her ears and a heavy presence at her shoulders assured her that he trailed after her at close range. "I'll be over at ten."

"That's fine." She suppressed the urge to ask him what the hell his problem was. He'd rejected her, not the other way around.

"I'll take the outside spot so I have plenty of room." Brenna pointed to the chair across from her. "Christy, why don't you go on that side? And Dad can sit between us."

Well, this should be fun.

Christy settled into the assigned seat and tried to prepare herself for the most uncomfortable evening of her life.

Sven huffed out a sigh, suggesting he wasn't any happier with the plan than she was. "Are you sure you fit okay there, Bee?"

"It's perfect." Brenna's barely noticeable smirk outed her amusement. Suddenly, her intentions were all too clear.

A matchmaking attempt.

CHAPTER SIX

Sven pushed a piece of pepper away from the edge of the cast-iron skillet, wishing he was anywhere other than sitting next to the woman he'd once expected to marry. Maybe if he kept his gaze on his plate and his mouth full of fajitas, Brenna would stop trying to find ways to make him talk to his former girlfriend. He wasn't interested in getting reacquainted with Christy Rime, his daughter's favorite person in the whole damn world. She'd left him and he'd given up on love—the romantic kind.

"Do you have plans for Christmas?" His daughter's question triggered another lead weight sinking into his gut, especially when the ball of tension radiating off their dinner companion wound tighter.

He refused to subject himself to any more of it. "Bee, do you need a box? We should get going. I have paperwork to do yet tonight."

She aimed a side-eye at him that told him she saw exactly what he was doing to cut the evening short. "Of course. How about you, Christy?"

Their guest gave a curt nod, making her wavy hair slide

over her shoulder. "Yes. It was good, but I guess I wasn't very hungry."

Don't look at her.

With more confidence than she'd shown since her injury, Brenna flagged down their waiter and requested boxes and a single check. "Before you protest, this is to thank you for practically giving me your house, the help when I was stuck in the street, the offer to be my OT, for being nice, and a bunch of other stuff. I can never repay you."

"I did what anybody would do." Christy shifted in her seat, clearly uncomfortable with the attention, but that wasn't why he was staring at her.

I'm weak and a glutton for punishment.

He struggled against the need to contradict her statement, but she truly deserved full credit. "They haven't done what you have. I'm paying."

Bee's smug expression tempted him to leave her holding the bill. His crumbling resolve was all her doing. "You're right. Thanks, Dad."

"Thank you." The quiet acknowledgment brought his focus back to his daughter's hero. She seemed focused on transferring most of her meal to the box next to her plate, completely unaware of his obsessive need to memorize every little detail about her.

At least he'd finally won a small victory, no small feat given his adversaries. "You're welcome."

When they parted at his truck a few minutes later, she hurried toward her car, her loose hair whipping in the cold wind. Once she climbed inside and closed the driver's door, he set to work helping Brenna into the passenger seat and loading the wheelchair in the bed. The task had become routine during the last several months.

As he rounded the rear bumper, he allowed himself a last

look across the parking lot. Brake lights cast a red glow behind Christy's car, and he waited for a foggy exhale from the tailpipe so he could go home and bury his thoughts in estimates, billing, and payroll—whatever it took to stop thinking about her.

The slow count of thirty passed with no sign of her leaving. Then she opened the door and put her booted feet on the pavement.

He held up his index finger in a just-a-second gesture to Bee and jogged to the far corner of the lot. "Is something wrong?"

Christy growled as she stood. "My car won't start. I turn the key and nothing happens. Not even a click. It can't be the battery since I replaced it in April."

"Sounds like you might have a bad starter." His still-bitter heart didn't justify making a woman wait alone in the dark for a tow. He packed up the ache to save for another day. "Come on. We'll give you a ride and you can call for road service in the morning."

She pursed her lips, waking the memory of their first real kiss and sending shockwaves through his body. "I'll walk."

"Like hell, you will. Creekside isn't overrun with crime, but it isn't as safe as it was thirty years ago, especially at night." He scowled for good measure and crossed his arms in front of his chest. If she sneered at his upcoming ace in the hole, he would resort to a fireman's carry. "Besides, Bee will hand me my ass on a platter if I let you walk home by yourself."

Her pretty mouth twitched, a sure sign she was holding in a laugh at his mostly true argument. "Fine."

He enjoyed the view while she retrieved her purse and the carryout box of leftovers from the other side of the center console. Her reasons for skipping town didn't matter to his reawakening hormones.

She was here.

He was here.

Picking up where they'd left off didn't seem like a bad idea. In fact, it sounded better with each passing moment.

"It's locked up, not that anybody can steal my car very easily. Let's go before I change my mind." She walked ahead of him to his pickup and used the running board to claim the seat behind Brenna.

He caught the tail end of her explanation as he slid behind the steering wheel.

His daughter groaned. "That stinks. It's a good thing we were still here. I bet my dad knows the best garage to have it towed to."

Christy's noncommittal hum said she may or may not want or heed his advice.

"So, Dad, would you mind dropping me off first? I got a text from work about a last-minute change to the design my boss is presenting tomorrow morning. I need to send the updated version to her ASAP."

He shifted into gear and swiveled to look out the back window, hoping for a glimpse of their guest's reaction. "As long as Ms. Rime isn't in a hurry."

Christy rolled her eyes so hard they should've landed on the floor. "Not a problem."

But calling you Ms. Rime instead of Christy is.

She'd started their game of pretend by calling him Mr. Carlsen. Did she expect him to behave like he knew her and blow their cover?

He flipped on his turn signal to exit the parking lot, caught between what he wanted and what was wise. "Work, it is then, Bee."

"Thanks, Christy. I really appreciate it." His daughter tapped on the screen of her phone, probably informing her boss to expect an email shortly. Her barely audible sigh set off his protective-father radar. "I think I'll go to bed after I'm done. My back's a little tight from the therapy session. I'm not used to the twisting and lifting I did today. Different movement and different muscles."

Christy leaned forward. "Be sure to do the stretches we talked about. They'll help reduce the risk of soreness in your lower back until you get in the habit of prep work and cooking from your chair."

The concern and compassion in her voice tipped the scales a little farther from wisdom, but he didn't dare use his tendency to hover over Brenna to offset stupidity. She hated when he bulldozed his way into her independence. "Do you have any pain pills left? Just in case."

"It doesn't hurt that much." She slipped her phone into her purse and leaned against the headrest. "It's just a twinge, Dad. Pinky promise."

A shot of warmth spread through his chest from the saying she'd made up because preschooler-Brenna had insisted she wasn't allowed to swear. The occasional curse word had snuck out of his mouth, earning him a reproachful glare from his little girl.

Silence descended during the short drive to the house he'd bought for them when she was six. The good memories had been drowned out by the strain of her accident this year, but they were finally starting to resurface after the interminable hiatus.

He parked in the driveway and left the engine running as he repeated the motions that gave her the freedom to go places and do things again. By the time she let herself in the house and he climbed back in the driver's side, Christy had moved to the front passenger seat.

Clearing his throat, he sorted through the mish-mash of thoughts and headed along the familiar route to the house she'd grown up in. "She was struggling to make progress before you stopped to help her last week. And now... You have no idea how much it means to her. To me."

"I think I might. It's why I love what I do." She didn't look his direction, but her reflection in the window next to her didn't give even a hint of what was going on in her head. She hadn't always been so closed up to him.

"Well, you're very good at it." As much as he'd like to ask her to stay in Creekside for his daughter's sake, he wasn't that much of a masochist. Being near her made him remember how good they'd been together and for each other.

And I still feel something for her, even after she went away without telling me why.

His grief and disappointment had faded somewhat during dinner, slowly being replaced by hope for a chance to rekindle their relationship. Was he an idiot for thinking it was possible?

Too soon, the half-mile drive ended at the darkest spot on the street. No light illuminated the front porch and no window glowed from within.

He shut off the engine and unbuckled his seatbelt. "I'll walk you to the door."

"You don't have to do that. I'll be fine." Despite her frequent use of the word, she didn't seem fine to him. She was tense and standoffish and too willing to depend only on herself.

"Humor me." He climbed out before she could argue and stalked around the front end to help her down. "Give me your hand. There's a big crack in the blacktop below the running board."

She glanced at him with something that resembled fear.

Why was everything so damn difficult between them now?

Swallowing the urge to give up, he reached out to her. "I was also hoping we could talk."

"We talked while we were eating." The set of her jaw reminded him how she would resort to logic whenever they'd disagreed about even the smallest thing.

He sucked in a deep breath and took the biggest chance of his life. "We've never talked about why I couldn't go with you."

Her eyes narrowed. "Didn't."

"What?" He waited for her to explain the confusing retort.

"*Didn't* go with me, not couldn't." Judging by her tone, her hackles were raised and extra stabby.

"How would *you* know since you didn't let me tell why I *couldn't*?" Out of patience, he scooped her up, shoved the door closed with his hip, and marched along the sidewalk to the steps.

"Put me down." Her low growl might've scared a guy who didn't know she wouldn't hurt a fly.

When she tried to wiggle free, he tightened his hold on her. "After you agree to have a conversation with me about this. I'm tired of wondering what the hell happened that you wouldn't give me five minutes to tell you my mom had been diagnosed with cancer."

She froze, the fight going out of her in an instant. "Oh my god, is she okay? She didn't..."

He lowered her to the porch floor and lit up the doorknob and deadbolt with his phone's flashlight, but he readied his booted foot in case she tried to close the door in his face. "Unlock it. I'll answer you once we're inside."

"You know I can just ask Brenna." After a few seconds of fiddling with her key, she turned the knob and motioned for him to go first. A lamp came on in the living room when she swept her hand along the wall.

"Are you ready to tell her our history? Because she'll figure it out. She's smart like that." He grasped her hand, tugged her in behind him, and closed out the cold. The same electrical charge zapped his fingers, even though he was prepared for it. "Mom's been cancer-free since about a year after the diagnosis. The doctor caught it early. Still, I was scared to death. I needed to be here, and you wanted me to leave. What was I supposed to do? I'd always known I could depend on you, but then you walked away. I felt like you abandoned me."

Finally being able to share his side of the story and to let her know how deeply she'd hurt him brought relief. The flash of grief on her face didn't bring the satisfaction he'd hoped it would.

She wilted against him, all the indignation and hostility gone. "I'm sorry. I didn't know."

Her body molded to his as he wrapped his arms around her. The simple apology cleared away the haze he'd lived in for so long, and he tucked a finger under her chin to meet her gaze. Words of forgiveness stuck in his throat at the sight of her parted lips. Unable to resist, he pressed a gentle kiss to the mouth he'd loved to worship.

She chased him when he eased back, dragging him closer for another light touch and then another.

He cupped her cheek and surrendered to a deeper kiss, tangling his tongue with hers. She tasted sweet from the bite of churro she'd eaten for dessert, but the kiss was an irresistible combination of pure sin and absolute heaven. How many times had he dreamed of this moment?

Too many to count, that was for damn sure.

Her fingers tunneled under his shirt, singeing the skin she made contact with a few inches above his button fly. His dick hardened in the snug confines of his jeans. It wasn't in the mood for teasing. Then she palmed his length, pouring fuel on the raging fire she'd lit.

He broke the kiss and buried his face in her neck. "I missed you."

When he nibbled a path to her ear, she arched closer. "I need to feel you."

A groan rumbled out of his throat as his cock pulsed in an attempt to give her what she wanted, what they both wanted. He hoisted her off the ground and carried her down the dark hall to her bedroom, where they'd fumbled through gifting their virginity to each other at seventeen.

Thin slivers of light filtered through the closed blinds, casting shadowy stripes across the twin bed he aimed for. He lowered her to the comforter, switched on the lamp, and stripped off the layers above his waist.

Her sweater, leggings, and everything underneath landed on the floor while he removed his boots. She stared up at him with her smooth skin and soft curves on full display.

Breathtaking.

He swallowed the compliment, not wanting to do anything to break the spell they'd created.

Condom.

His heart pounded in his chest as he finished unfastening the last button and reached for his back pocket. Thank god, he always kept a fresh one in his wallet, not that he'd needed protection for almost a decade. A single stupid decision had taught him the replacement lesson well.

He pulled the foil packet from the money slot and performed a thorough inspection. Thankfully, the wrapper showed no signs of wear and tear.

She traced the trail of hair leading into his jeans, making his abs tense and his erection work harder to free itself. Her fingertips caressed his hipbones when she pushed the denim and his boxer briefs downward. Only the incredible elation at being touched by her after all this time stopped him from taking over the task and getting down to business. If she wanted to undress him, he would willingly submit to it.

At her prompting, he stepped out of his jeans and underwear, leaving them both naked. Her nipples puckered in the cool air. Or maybe she was remembering how he used to lick and suck them until she begged him to love her hard and fast. The F-word hadn't been part of her vocabulary, but loving her described their physical relationship far more accurately.

She reached out to him as she lay back on the tiny bed.

It was an invitation he couldn't refuse. He didn't care about risking his heart again for such a priceless opportunity. The memory of their intimate reunion would last a lifetime, no matter how much time they had together.

Condom first.

Stretching out beside her, he linked his fingers with hers and leaned in to kiss her, first with a light touch and then with all the emotion he'd bottled up over the years. Each desperate stroke of her tongue added to the instant heat lying skin to skin with her created.

When she let him up for air, he nuzzled her throat and licked a path toward her breasts. The gentle swell of their fullness drew him down her body to the tight buds he longed to taste. He circled the left tip with his tongue and the right with his finger before closing his lips around her nipple and sucking on her flesh.

Her breath hitched, encouraging him to continue his exploration. "More."

The huskiness of her voice went straight to his dick, but he focused on pleasuring her with his hands and mouth.

She clutched at his head, digging her short fingernails of one hand into his scalp as she whimpered. Her other hand glided from his bicep to his upper back. "I need you."

But do you want me? And for how long?

Those were the million-dollar questions he shouldn't even be asking.

He flicked across the taut tip in his mouth and released it to scoot down to her belly. If his time with her was limited, he would damn well enjoy every second of it. "Soon."

His exploration continued over more of her silky skin and toward a tastier treat than the churros they ordered. The sweet scent of desire coaxed him to the end of the bed to settle between her gorgeous thighs. He pressed a dozen kisses from her knee to the edge of her dark curls and blew a warm breath over his intended target.

"*Please.*" She shifted her hips, finding his chin instead of his lips.

There's the magic word.

He closed his mouth over her for the ultimate kiss and swept his tongue through her wetness. Near the top, he found her clit, ready and waiting for him. A few seconds of intense flutters earned him the reaction he wanted—an orgasm paired with a high-pitched cry. A quick switch to hard sucking prolonged the spasms and triggered a choked scream.

Her legs trembled as he kissed her inner thighs. Tiny tremors pulsed through her body on his return trip to her stomach, her nipples, and finally her parted lips.

Positioning his sheathed cock at her entrance, he locked his gaze on her hers. "Are you sure?"

CHAPTER SEVEN

REELING FROM THE ORAL SATISFACTION SVEN HAD INSISTED on giving her, Christy could only nod to confirm she was very sure she needed the physical connection to him.

He kissed her forehead, the tip of her nose, and then her lips as he slipped inside her, inch by unhurried inch. His beard stubble scratched her chin, but the sensation reminded her he was real.

She gasped when he bottomed out.

"You okay?" He'd been a considerate lover, always mindful of her comfort during their lovemaking.

She swallowed to wet her prickly throat. "Much better than okay."

"Slow and easy or fast and hard? I should warn you. Either way, I won't last long." He withdrew partway and rocked forward until he was back where he belonged. His low groan rumbled through her jaw. "You feel so damn good."

"Slow for a few minutes. I want to savor it." *In case I never get to experience it again.* She wrapped her legs around his waist and pulled him deeper still. The motion stole her breath again. Cradling his scruffy jaw in her palm, she lifted her head to kiss him.

His leisurely in-and-out glide matched the slide of his tongue with hers. The coordinated dance made the world fall away, lifting her to a new plane of existence. He combed his fingers through her hair and caressed her cheek with calloused fingertips, touching and loving her like his sole purpose was to bring her pleasure. Her mind cleared and her body floated on a cloud of utter decadence and euphoria.

She let her hands wander over the contours of his muscled arms and back, certain she could die the most sexually satisfied woman in the world right here, right now.

Then his lips grazed her jaw and his rough exhales bathed her neck in warmth. He didn't speak, but she didn't need words or promises, only this union.

After another restrained rock of his hips, a pained growl brought an end to the measured pace he'd set. "I can't... I need to... Hold on to me."

His warning didn't prepare her for the sudden barrage of sensations that flooded her nerve endings. Each thrust carried her higher than the one before, sending her heart, body, and soul into freefall. A guttural roar echoed off the walls as he stiffened above her and throbbed inside her.

Her pulse thumped in her ears, telling her she was more alive than she'd ever felt before.

He dropped to his elbows, blanketing her with his body, anchoring her with his weight. The steady pressure calmed her racing heartbeat, but doubts and warnings invaded her thoughts.

"You're thinking too loud." His gruff comment sparked a tiny surge of guilt. He shifted to his side and then onto his back, taking her with him. Somehow, he managed to keep them from falling off the bed. His partially deflated erection had slipped free during their rearrangement, and the loss was profound. Guiding her head to his chest, he tugged the comforter over top of her. Despite having his arms around her and the leveling heartbeat in her ear, tension rolled off of him in massive waves. "I can't stay. Brenna might need me and she'll want to know what took so long as it is."

"It's fine." She didn't expect anything from him because they'd had sex—not promises, not commitments, or even an offer to do it again. Emotional involvement and expectations weren't part of the unspoken agreement.

"I hate that word." He brought her hand to his lips and kissed each finger. "Will you have supper with me tomorrow?"

More than a little relieved to already have plans, she sent up a silent thank-you to his daughter for roping her into playing Mrs. Claus. "I'll be busy all day tomorrow."

Why did the truth seem like an excuse?

"Oh. Okay." He sounded disappointed, but she refused to let her guilty conscience make her do something stupid. "I want to see you again, in case I wasn't clear about that. Tonight wasn't about getting naked with you."

She rolled out of his arms and sat on the edge of the bed with her back to him. The urge to escape hit much quicker than usual. "I'm leav—"

"I'm asking you to stay, at least long enough to give us a chance." The bed shifted behind her, but he didn't touch her. "Bee's mother was the first woman I was with after you. I thought I could find someone else. Not even a month into dating, she said I was emotionally unavailable and dumped me. Two years after you went away, I still couldn't move on from you. I'm older now, but wiser remains to be seen since I plan to fight for you this time if I have to."

His declaration hung in the air between them, inciting panic, fear, hope, and too many other reactions to process.

She hunched her shoulders, wishing she could disappear. Hiding her true self had become second nature, and he'd somehow cut through the façade without her realizing it.

The rustle of clothes was punctuated by a sigh. Then footsteps trudged toward the hall and a door clicked shut. The muffled shoosh of water followed, suggesting he'd gone to the bathroom to dispose of the condom and get dressed.

Goosebumps nudged her into motion, and she quickly donned her flannel pajamas and fluffy robe. As she slid her bare feet into her slippers, the heavy tread of boots broke the silence. Fighting her heart's desire to turn around, she focused on gathering her clothes from the floor.

In her peripheral vision, he loomed in the bedroom doorway. "Being in this house and going through your father's things has to be tough, but I'm here if you want to talk and if you're ready to tell me why you needed to get out. Day or night. I'll see you soon, I hope."

His gentle voice tempted her to look up at him, but she didn't trust herself to stick to her resolve. "Nothing has changed."

"*Everything* has changed." His frustrated tone battered the walls she'd reconstructed. "He's dead. He can't treat you like you don't exist anymore. And I'm still here. You matter, Christy. You've always mattered to me. Doesn't that count for something?"

Unshed tears stung her eyes, but she blinked them away. "You don't understand."

"No, I don't understand why you—"

"I just can't." She wrapped her arms around herself, in hopes of holding the pieces together. "Please go."

"For now. I'll wait on the porch for you to lock up behind

me." The purposeful *thud, thud, thud* of him walking away hammered at her intent to keep her distance.

Having sex with him had been a mistake, whether her body thought so or not.

She waited until his footsteps ended and a clunk sounded to follow him. Armed with a tissue to combat the wetness trying to leak onto her cheeks, she shuffled to the living room. The ancient floor lamp beside the old recliner flickered and went out a few steps from her destination.

Of course, the bulb burns out now.

Sven's face came into focus through the six-pane window in the door. He frowned and his eyebrows dipped toward his nose, but he didn't move.

He saw me crying.

If he knew how difficult pushing him away was, would he use that knowledge to his advantage?

Lowering her head, she stepped close enough to turn the deadbolt and then the lock on the knob. As metaphors went, locking him out seemed like a good one, even when part of her didn't want to.

Her gaze strayed upward without her permission as she started to turn, catching sight of a fogged pane in the bottom row. *I ♡ U* filled the steamed-up square.

The simple message woke memories of him doing the same thing on her bedroom window hundreds of times. He'd rarely let a cold day go by without telling her how much she meant to him that way.

On the verge of bawling, she rushed toward her bedroom. Halfway there, she detoured to the dark bathroom and shut herself inside. Sleeping would be impossible with his presence lingering in her personal space and his masculine scent clinging to the pillows and blankets. Another night in her father's room with his indifference haunting her wasn't an option, either.

The couch? The bathtub? My car?

She sat on the toilet lid and buried her face in her hands. Returning to Creekside, even temporarily, had been a disastrous decision. The man who'd barely tolerated her existence should've named someone else—anyone else—his beneficiary.

The low hum of an engine outside the bathroom window, the crunch of gravel, and the flash of headlights across the wall announced Sven's departure. Only near-darkness and her gasping sobs remained. Instead of bringing relief, being completely alone pushed her to the edge of despair.

Not once since she'd packed her suitcase and bought a bus ticket to Cleveland had she surrendered to grief. She'd fought tooth and nail to stay strong and forget the past. Her life had consisted of working in the library, going to class, studying, and squeezing in a few hours of sleep when she couldn't keep her eyes open. She'd been self-reliant and self-sufficient by necessity as much as choice.

Her mindset hadn't allowed anything to change during her internships or numerous jobs after graduating twice—stay busy, help her patients, and move on when the time felt right. She'd faltered twice. Her body, if not her heart, had betrayed her. Two kind men had convinced her to give them a chance, leading to adequate sex and a pair of marriage proposals that had ended soon after. Neither breakup had been painful or terribly disappointing.

Sven wanted her to show her entire self to him, including all the broken parts she'd had to acknowledge during her most-recent attempt to find peace. The psychologist had subtly convinced her to find closure in Creekside, but being here had reopened old wounds rather than healing them.

Too exhausted to continue rehashing her ghastly history with interpersonal and familial relationships, she trudged to the couch, curled up in the corner farthest from the recliner, and dropped her forehead to her knees. Only her professional acquaintances had brought normalcy to her life since she'd become an adult, but that was at risk with her association with Brenna.

After tomorrow's fundraiser, Mrs. Claus would turn back into a pumpkin to finalize settling Walter Rime's estate, pack up her few belongings, and make a quiet exit. Self-preservation would save her again.

HOLDING ON TO HER WIG AND BONNET, CHRISTY HURRIED along the vaguely familiar corridor, the *click, click, click* of her black lace-up ankle boots echoing off the walls. Despite last night's turmoil, she'd fallen into a deep sleep and awakened to bright sunshine forty-five minutes before Claus for a Cause and Mrs. Claus's Cookie Kitchen were set to welcome patrons. A quick shower and a lot more makeup than usual later, she'd put on her costume in the faculty restroom near the main office and hightailed it to the other side of the building.

It's a good thing I have lots of practice pretending to be happy.

As she approached the old Home Ec. room from her high school days, Brenna rounded the corner not far beyond the classroom entrance, clad in a green tunic and candy-cane striped leggings. Red pointy-toes slippers matched the outfit. Her long strokes propelled her along the straightaway much faster than Christy could run in her heels. She coasted the last several yards, adjusting her Santa hat as her chair slowed.

"You look amazing! Thanks again for agreeing to help with the cookie decorating and pictures. You really saved the day."

"Glad to help." Christy followed her guide into the festively decorated space. Luckily, the wire-rimmed glasses she wore didn't have lenses to blur the lighted snowflakes hanging from the ceiling or the strands of white lights framing the windows. Round tables with red-and-green plaid tablecloths were set with laminated placemats, child-sized butter knives, small tubs of colored frosting, and shakers of sprinkles. More supplies were organized on a long counter at the back of the room. The aroma of freshly baked sugar cookies filled the air. Not until she'd lived on her own had she associated the smell with Christmas. "How did you not have a hundred volunteers for this job?"

Brenna's genuine laughter added to the ambience. "Mrs. Barber has claimed it for as long as I've been alive, and I needed a substitute in a hurry. You were in the right place at the right time. The bakers will be wheeling out trays of cookies at ten on the dot and your helpers will be arriving any minute. Text me if you have any questions. Ten minutes until the invasion. I'm off to check on the craft room, the toy workshop, and the retail shop. And I need to text Santa to be sure he and the outdoor elves are ready to pass out pellets to feed to the reindeer."

An involuntary shiver raced through her. "Brr. It's cold out there today. Better them than me."

Brenna grinned and pivoted toward the doorway. "Right? See you at lunch. Ten after twelve in the teachers' lounge. You have a thirty-minute break starting at noon, so don't be late!"

"Got it. Time for a stop in the restroom and a quick bite to eat." Christy saluted her supervisor. "I'll save a cookie for you."

"Ha! I already snagged one from the kitchen before you got here, but thanks for thinking of me. You're the best." Brenna glanced over her shoulder with a sweet smile exactly like her father's. Then she zipped into the hallway and out of sight.

Ignoring the knot in the pit of her stomach, Christy crossed to the supply counter to familiarize herself with the setup. Low voices carried into the room from the corridor, and she braced for the first test of her disguise.

A trio of women sashayed into the Cookie Kitchen, dressed more for a night of clubbing and hookups than a morning of frosting and nonpareils. Their gold, silver, and black sequined halter tops caught and reflected the light from the snowflakes. All three aimed death stares at her as they continued past the tables.

The blonde in the middle stopped and the others followed suit, like they'd never matured past the high school cliques they'd obviously been a part of. "Who did you sleep with? Was it Sven?"

Hmm. I know that screechy voice.

Thoroughly confused by the woman's question, Christy set down the tub of icing she'd picked up and mentally crossed her fingers the popular girls weren't the volunteers Brenna had mentioned. "I have no idea what you're talking about."

Their spokesperson pursed her blood-red lips and narrowed her spider-lashed eyes. "How did you get the job of Mrs. Claus? There's a waiting list for when Mrs. Barber dies or can't do it anymore, and I'm pretty sure you're not on it. I've never seen you before, so you must not be from Creekside."

Well, I've seen you, and you haven't changed a bit.

Determined to hide her identity from the snobs who'd

tried to bully her from kindergarten to graduation, Christy stood her ground. "I don't know anything about a waiting list, but I was asked by one of the organizers and it was okayed by Mrs. Barber. Are you here to help with the cookie decorating?"

"What? No, of course not!" The former homecoming queen scrunched up her nose and lifted her chin. "I'm in charge of the retail shop, the biggest moneymaker of the—"

"Sorry, we're late!" Two girls and two boys who looked to be college-aged rushed through the door. The shorter of the young women whipped off her ski jacket. "The dog threw up, my tights got a hole in them, and then there was a traffic jam where they're fixing the pothole at the intersection in front of Lorenzo's. I'm Anna. My friends are Isaiah, Grace, and Byron. Hey, Mrs. Potter. You look…different. Did you have some work done?"

The look the mean-girls ringleader leveled at Anna should've turned her to ash.

"Oh, and the principal is looking for you. He said to tell you to get down to the store right now if we saw you."

Whirling on her no-doubt designer shoes, the blonde bully motioned for her cohorts to follow her. "Don't think this is the end of it. I'm going to have a talk with the mayor."

Anna snorted as the trio made their grand exit. "Talk? More like do the nasty with. I swear she's cheated on her husband with every willing guy in town."

Christy extended her hand to her savior, hoping to conclude that topic. "I'm Mrs. Claus. It's nice to meet you. Thanks for volunteering."

The young man with glasses unzipped his coat and shrugged it off. "Brenna was always nice to us in school, even though we were three years behind her. We're happy to help with the fundraiser whatever way we can."

"Who's collecting tickets? There's a bucket here with the extra frosting and sprinkles." Christy stepped aside to let her helpers stow their winterwear by the storage closet. Rattling alerted her to the first cookie delivery from the connected kitchenettes next door and the imminent arrival of their patrons. "The Cookie Kitchen opens for business in two minutes."

A steady stream of children, teenagers, and adults kept her and her team busy for the entire two-hour slot, and the full bucket suggested a decent number of residents had shown up to support the event, the community, and one of their own.

She boxed up the few remaining cookies, added what was left of the frosting and sprinkles, and set it on the cart the bakers would retrieve soon. The rest of the crew had promised to take care of table cleanup so she could grab lunch and a potty break before pictures with her make-believe husband.

After a last scan of the room, she picked up the bucket of counted tickets by the handle and headed for the door. "Thank you so much for volunteering. You were great with the kids *and* the parents. Be sure to stop by the hot cocoa booth tonight. My treat."

"Thanks!" All four of her elves sang out their appreciation in unison.

Anna dumped a placemat of sprinkles into the trashcan and grinned. "You make an awesome Mrs. Claus. I hope the Cause Committee asks you to do it again next year. See you tonight!"

Offering a noncommittal nod, Christy turned left into the corridor. She wouldn't be here next year to play the role she'd been roped into by Brenna. She wasn't even sure about going to tonight's festivities. A spark of regret burned in her stomach, but staying wasn't part of her plan. It never had been.

Get in. Get the job done. Get out.

That was her mantra.

She stayed in character on the brisk walk to the opposite side of the building. When the coast was clear, she checked her phone to see if she had time for a restroom stop before lunch.

12:08. Food first. I'll just have to eat fast.

Brenna rolled into the hallway as Christy hurried toward the teachers' lounge. "You didn't get lost, did you?"

Holding up the bucket, Christy shook her head. "We still had a few people in line at noon and I wanted to make sure everyone got to decorate a cookie. Here are the tickets. One of the helpers counted them."

"Thank you, thank you, thank you." Brenna reached for the handle. "I'll take that. Go eat while you can."

"You're welcome." Grateful for the short break, Christy headed into the mostly empty room and straight to the table of boxed lunches. She chose the turkey wrap option, pulled a bottled water from the small refrigerator, and sat facing the window.

The silence lasted only a few seconds before Brenna greeted whoever was impersonating the main attraction. "Hey, Santa. Help yourself to the free food. There're drinks too. Coffee, iced and hot tea, water. Twenty minutes until wishes and pictures."

A heavy sigh warned Christy that Santa wasn't in a very jolly mood. "Kids only. *No. Adults.*"

Her pulse stuttered at the unexpected voice.

Sven Carlsen was Santa Claus.

CHAPTER EIGHT

HOPING HIS DAUGHTER FOLLOWED THROUGH ON HER PROMISE, Sven refilled his insulated mug with coffee and added two creamers before moving down to the stack of lunches. He tucked a box under his arm, picked up his drink, and stalked to the seat across from Janice Barber in her Mrs. Claus outfit.

She didn't look up when he sat, evidently entranced by the package of sliced apples. The wrapper crinkled in her grasp—fingers that were decidedly not those of an eighty-something-year-old woman.

Mrs. Barber hadn't missed Claus for a Cause since she'd been given the role at least thirty years ago, so having a replacement was a big deal.

He tried and failed to get a look at her stand-in's face to see who had replaced his sixth grade English teacher this year. The imposter wore a snowy white wig, something her predecessor had never needed. A pair of gold-rimmed glasses rested on the bridge of her nose and the ruffly collar of her dress came up to her chin.

She swapped the apples for another package about the same size, but she didn't open it.

She has to look up sometime.

Stifling his curiosity, he lifted both flaps on the top of the box and pulled out his sandwich. As he loosened the wrapper, his lunch companion finally shifted enough for him to catch a glimpse of a rosy cheek. The color seemed unnatural, like she'd used some sort of makeup to create the pink glow that matched her down-turned lips. Considering how she was ignoring him, the chances of her being one of the previous schemers were slim. They'd all flaunted their bodies and flirted within an inch of their lives, in hopes of bagging the bachelor who they thought liked to play hard to get.

Not interested is more like it.

The woman he wanted was making him work for it—with no guaranteed prize at the end.

He bit his sandwich, chewing a little more vigorously than necessary. Christy hadn't answered her phone this morning when he'd called to make arrangements for her car to be towed and repaired. However, no transportation meant she couldn't leave town yet.

I need more time.

To do what?

He had no secret weapon to convince her to stay. Asking her had gotten him nowhere. Promising to fight for her hadn't done any good. Telling her he loved her—in writing—had sent her fleeing into the dark.

Mrs. Claus scraped her chair away from the table as she returned most of her wrap, the package of apples, and the mini bag of pretzels to the box. Without a word, she turned her back to him and scurried out of the room, her candy-cane print dress swishing around her ankles. Murmurs from the hallway suggested she'd spoken to his daughter during her quick exit.

This afternoon's activities should be loads of fun. The

woman can't even say hello to the guy she's pretending to be married to.

Ho.

Ho.

Ho.

He finished his meal with eight minutes to spare and set off for the closest restroom to check his beard for crumbs and prepare for a three-hour shift at the center of attention with no break. After an adjustment to his padding and belt and a last check in the mirror, he marched to the gymnasium.

The crowd of kids and adults Brenna had told him to expect waited outside the set of double doors at the far end of the space, their laughter and chatter carrying to the throne-like seat reserved for him. A fake fir tree about twice his height stood behind it, its lights reflecting off the silver bells scattered throughout the branches. ENTER HERE and EXIT HERE signs hung from chains on either side of the roped off area, but he was less concerned about crowd control than women on the prowl.

As he sat in the chair, his less-than-talkative other half walked through the same side door he'd used a few paces behind a pair of burly teenagers. Each boy hefted a large basket and blocked most of his view of Mrs. Claus. Only her low-heeled boots that clicked in a steady clip-clop, clip-clop on the polished floor were visible except the lower part of her full skirt.

He braced for the cold shoulder again when her over-grown elves set down their loads near the tree. Wasn't she supposed to be a nice lady who loved kids, the holiday season, and cookies?

"Thank you so much for helping. Stop by the cider booth later for one on me." Her sickening sweet voice grated on his nerves.

The taller of the two guys grinned. "Cool. Thanks, Mrs. C."

His partner nodded. "Yeah, thanks. Let us know if you need more help carrying stuff."

"I will. Thanks again." When the boys tromped off toward the same door they'd come in, she straightened the ribbons on the baskets and then faked being busy by straightening the wrapped gifts for each kid who shared a wish list or was brave enough to try.

Completely ignoring me.

Whatever.

Sven scratched at the elastic beneath his hat, ready for this day to be done so he could focus on wooing Christy. She hadn't returned his call, not that he'd left a voicemail message or thought she would. The emotional overload and his handling of it had obviously scared the hell out of her, but last night's reunion had been like waking up after dying. Their connection was still there, soul-deep and stronger than ever.

I know she felt it too.

The thundering footsteps and excited voices of a huge herd of kids and parents entering the gym put an end to his ruminating. A line formed, starting at the entrance to his makeshift cage and ending somewhere beyond the double doors. The elf positioned at the chain reached for the clip and raised her eyebrows at him.

He nodded once and the photographer did the same.

Be jolly.

Brenna's earlier admonition rang through his head when the first little girl handed his ticket to the elf and dragged a harried-looking woman toward him. He'd repaired part of their roof sometime during the spring and she'd invited him to a tea party with her stuffed animal friends.

"Hi, Thanta! I wath exthra good thith year!"

Her enthusiasm and missing top front tooth sparked a twinge of melancholy. He missed that stage, despite how much he'd had to rely on his mom and dad to help him raise his young daughter.

His visitor extended both arms in the universal pick-me-up gesture, prompting him to lift her onto his lap. "I know you were, Iona. You helped your mom and dad with the twins when they were born and made cookies for your grandpa."

Her eyes widened, likely because he threw in details only an omniscient fictional being would know. "I did!"

"I can't promise to bring all the presents you want, but you're welcome to tell me what's on your Christmas list this year." He leaned down so she could whisper in his ear.

"Bookth I can read all by mythelf to my little brotherth." Between her toothlessness and her excitement, she sprayed a few droplets of spit on his neck, but he'd experienced a lot worse when Brenna was a baby. "Pleath and thank you."

Touched by her sweet demeanor, he sat up and winked at her. "I'll see what I can do about that. Do you want to have your picture taken with me?"

Her orangey-red curls bounced up and down when she nodded. She smiled in the direction of the camera until the photographer gave her a thumbs-up. Then she flung her arms around him and kissed his cheek. "Merry Chrithmas, Thanta!"

"Merry Christmas, Iona. Be sure to stop and say hi to Mrs. Claus. I think she has a gift for you." He stood her on the floor and waved her mother across in front of him to follow the girl to the baskets by the exit. Instead of immediately greeting the next kid, he waited for his counterpart to do her thing.

Turning toward Iona, Mrs. Claus greeted her with a

welcoming smile and handed her one of the wrapped pack-
ages. They exchanged a few words before his fake wife cast a
glance toward him, finally allowing him a good look at her
face. It was one he knew well, especially those eyes that
never quite hid the pain of her childhood.

Christy.

That explained her standoffish behavior during their lunch
break.

His heart thudded double-time in his chest for several
beats.

*She's here. She didn't run away. Yet. I just need to get
through being the guy in the red suit for a few hours. Then I'll
try to talk to her again.*

She whirled away, focusing her attention on the little girl
and her mother, but not before he caught the panic that shut
him out. After Iona hugged her around the waist, she fussed
in the basket, even though it couldn't possibly need
straightening.

She's going to run as soon as she can.

If she truly didn't feel the same about him as he did
about her, he would let her go. It might rip his heart out of
his chest, but he'd already survived nearly two-thirds of his
life without her. Fortunately, his gut told him she still loved
him too and needed a little more reassurance to tip the
balance.

A light tug on his sleeve brought his focus back to his job.
"'Scuse me, Santa. It's my turn, and I have questions."

The task at hand took precedence at the moment, so he
rested his elbows on his knees to give the next visitor his full
attention. "I'll do my best to answer them."

For the rest of his shift, he tried not to glance at Christy or
the line that seemed to go on forever while he listened to
wishes and endured the tricky quest for inside information

about his workshop, the flying reindeer, and a dozen other topics related to his gig at the North Pole.

He caught his daughter watching him from the other side of the velvet rope several times. Her obvious joy more than made up for dealing with a few greedy kids and some pushy parents.

As the last toddler patted his fake beard and giggled, the photographer snapped a picture and gestured that it was a good one.

Brenna's laughter rang out in the background noise of people milling around the large booth where they could view and purchase the photos. Hearing that sound made his whole year. After spending most of it healing from her injuries, learning how to live in a world that wasn't very accommodating, and trying to fit in with friends who now treated her differently, she seemed happy again.

And all of the festival is for her.

His gaze drifted in the direction of the sound, but it stuck on the woman handing out the dozen or so gifts she had left to the elf helpers. A wide smile lit up Christy's face, reminding him why he'd always been drawn to her—from their first day of kindergarten together to this moment. She went out of her way to share her thoughtfulness, even when she had little to be happy about.

"Hey, Santa! Mrs. Claus!" The photographer waved them toward her. "I need you over here for the official website photo."

Sven waited for Christy to make the first move and then followed her to the pine-and-ribbon clad trellis. A sprig of green leaves with white berries hung from the top of the arch, tempting him to put it to good use. The Clauses were married, so a chaste kiss under the mistletoe in public would be family friendly.

Technically, he should ask her for permission, but they'd gone beyond a simple lip-lock last night—and it had shaken him awake. If he didn't do his damnedest to resurrect their relationship, regrets would dog him for the rest of his life.

She stopped, stiff-spined and tense-jawed, at the arbor outside the roped-off area and pivoted toward the woman with the camera. Her hands were clutched in front of her. She might not know for sure that he'd recognized her, but she knew for sure he was playing Santa today.

As soon as he stood beside her, the photographer motioned for them to move toward the center. "You need to squeeze close together inside the arch. Back just a little farther. Angle in a bit, but not quite face to face. Right there. Santa, hold Mrs. Claus's hands in yours. Now look at each other with that magic Christmas sparkle in your eyes. Smiles. Perfect. Don't move."

A familiar electrical current charged through him with the first contact and amped up when she finally looked at him. The surrounding noise faded away and only the two of them existed. Unable to resist, he caressed her cheek and leaned in. A tentative brush of his lips against her softer ones became a gentle caress and then a firm press when she whimpered loud enough for only him to hear. Her lips parted, inviting him inside, and he didn't hesitate to take their kiss to the next level with a slow stroke of his tongue.

At the clearing of a throat, he reluctantly eased back, taking in the undeniable desire in her stare. The beginnings of fear started to show through the lusty haze, urging him into action. "I love you, Christy. Please stay. Marry me."

CHAPTER NINE

SVEN'S BUSHY WHITE EYEBROWS DIPPED LOW AND HIS BEARD-framed mouth flattened into a thin line. "I'll do whatever it takes to convince you to stay and I'm not changing my mind about the marriage proposal, so say you'll think about it. Or you could just say yes."

Every cell in Christy's body ceased functioning for what seemed like an eternity. Despite the warmth of his skin around her fingers, she seemed to have lost all feeling. She couldn't breathe, couldn't think, couldn't move—except her knees, which decided to give out.

"You need to breathe."

When she couldn't force out a response, he scooped her into his arms and carried her to the chair he'd used during the visit-with-Santa segment. He sat, still cradling her to his chest and looking like he was contemplating a call to the on-site emergency crew.

She finally managed to suck in a slow breath. "I—"

"Do I need to alert the EMTs? Is she okay?" Brenna's concerned voice cut through the weird buzzing in Christy's ears. "What happened?"

His slightly rosy cheeks grew redder. "She was feeling woozy. Can you have somebody get her something to drink?"

The photographer reached past Brenna in her wheelchair, holding out a bottled water. "They started kissing under the mistletoe while I was taking pictures and then she looked like she was going to faint."

"You were *kissing*?" His daughter's half whispered question rose an octave with every word.

Sven grabbed the bottle and twisted off the cap. "Here. Take a few sips."

The worry in his eyes faded a little as she drank two swallows, but the shock inspired by his unexpected request lingered in her confused brain.

Brenna rolled closer and spoke low enough not to be overheard by the crowd still gathered in the gym. "Are you planning to answer my question? Not that I have a problem with it. I'd just kind of like to know if you're dating my OT."

He capped the bottle without looking at his daughter. His gaze seemed permanently locked on hers, setting off that lightheaded feeling again. "I'll date her if I have to, but I'd rather marry her. Maybe you could put in a good word for me since she likes you, Bee?"

"Wha— Oh my god. Of course!" Brenna sounded more excited than any of the kids who'd sat on Santa's lap. "Christy, listen to me. I know he's a little grumpy sometimes, but I promise he's loyal and kind and reliable and he loves with his whole heart."

The fake beard wiggled, as did his hat, when he shook his head. "I'm not a dog."

"Hush, Dad. I'm not finished. Now, where was I?" His daughter frowned for a moment before forging ahead. "Oh yeah. And you must be incredibly special to him, because he's never asked anybody to marry him before. I don't think he's even been on a date in years. Or maybe my entire life."

Christy didn't believe the last speculation, but the fact that Brenna hadn't met any of his dates meant something.

"Oh, something else. My dad is definitely not a love-at-first-sight kind of person, which means the two of you have a history—probably from when you lived here. I wouldn't be at all surprised if you've known each other since kindergarten and were high school sweethearts. You might not have grown up in the digital age, but information is pretty easy to find on the internet if you know where to look." A smug grin created a pair of shallow but visible dimples in the young woman's cheeks. "Am I right?"

Sven grunted, clearly unwilling to confirm her guesses with an outright yes.

"And, Dad, did you actually *ask* Christy to marry you? Or did you do that thing where you make it sound like an exasperated command? A ring would probably make your proposal more sincere too. I'm going to check in with the ticket committee. Text me when you're officially engaged." Brenna wheeled away, evidently finished with her insightful guesses and unsolicited advice.

He tightened his hold around Christy's waist and sighed. "I swear she's a bigger know-it-all now than she ever was as a teenager. Sadly, she's also almost always right. I should've asked you instead of sounding desperate and bossy. Do you mind if we get out of here so we can have a little privacy?"

Hope tried to take root again, but she smothered it. If she told him the secret that had sent her fleeing years ago, maybe he would understand why she wasn't cut out for relationships.

THE SEA OF CREEKSIDE RESIDENTS PARTED AS SVEN ESCORTED Christy to the gymnasium's double doors. Their smirks and winks told him word of the very public mistletoe kiss and Mrs. Claus's subsequent swooning had spread like wildfire.

He tangled his fingers with hers to keep her from making a break for the teachers' lounge or the parking lot without him. Carrying her had been his first choice, but she probably would've strangled him if he'd tried. Thankfully, his hard-on from holding her on his lap hid behind the hem of his fur-trimmed red coat.

She tried to tug her hand free when they finally emerged from the crowd and grumbled when he didn't release her. "Where are we going?"

"To the nurse's office." Dodging an elf carrying a box, he narrowed the space between him and his make-believe better half.

"I don't need medical attention."

"No, but we need a quiet place with no chance of inter-ruption so we can have a serious discussion that should've happened a long time ago." A sign for his destination pointed to the right, amplifying the nervous tension in his neck and shoulders. This would be his do-or-die moment.

She didn't drag her feet or argue that they had nothing to talk about, which were both positive signs.

The key the school secretary had loaned him slid into the lock with no resistance, saving him from having to text her for assistance getting into the room right outside the main office. He flipped on the light, gestured to the empty chair, and closed the door behind them. "Let's sit."

Although she didn't look terribly pleased to be trapped in the tight space with him, she settled into the seat and calmly folded her hands in her lap. Her white knuckles betrayed her calm exterior.

He moved his street clothes from the second chair to the counter and turned his seat to face hers. As much as he needed to pace, he sat instead. "I still love you, Christy. For a while, I was so hurt I thought I hated you, but I couldn't help it. No matter how hard I tried to wish the feeling away, it was always there. I gave up fighting it after a while and resigned myself to being alone for the rest of my life and focused on being a good father. Do you still love me?"

She stared at him without blinking for what seemed like a full minute. "My feelings for you are irrel—"

"No, they aren't." Despite wanting to vent about her worthless father's influence on her self-image, he swallowed the harsh rant that wouldn't make any difference since the jackass was dead. "Your feelings matter to me."

Her hands clenched tighter, making him yearn to wrap them in his. "Fine. Yes, but—"

"No buts." His heart sang with the knowledge that she hadn't lost the intense connection he struggled with twenty-seven years later. "We're taking this one step at a time. Okay?"

She nodded, even though she looked like she wanted to be anywhere but here.

Relieved to have her cooperation, he sorted through his jumbled thoughts. "Will you consider staying? I know Creek-side has a lot of painful memories for you. We made so many good ones, though. Our friendship. All the things we did together. Falling in love. I want to make new memories with you, like loving you last night and kissing you under the mistletoe just now."

"But..." Tears shone in her eyes, and they were like a punch to his solar plexus. "The day I left... It was all a lie. I found a legal document, two letters, and a picture by accident when I was looking for a book in my father's bedroom. My mother didn't die in childbirth. She signed away her parental rights and gave him full custody of me. My grandparents forced him to keep me when he wanted to turn me over to the state. Then they grudgingly let me stay at their house over winter break every year. None of them wanted me. How was I supposed to stay here?"

"Son of a bitch." Rage coursed through him, even as he hauled her into his arms and wrapped himself around her, wishing he'd been able to protect her. He'd known her family situation wasn't anything like his, but he hadn't realized how shitty it was until her revelation. "I'm so damn sorry. They didn't deserve to know you. If you stay with me, I promise you'll never question if you're wanted. Not another second for as long as you live. I love you and I've always wanted you. Please stay. Be part of my family. Will you marry me, Christy?"

She buried her face in his chest. Quiet sobs shook her shoulders and ripped his soul to shreds. At least she wasn't pushing him away anymore.

He tightened his hold on her and rubbed her back in slow circles, hoping like hell he was providing her some comfort. "I'm here. No matter what you decide, I'm here for you."

His phone buzzed in his pocket, but he refused to let the outside world intrude on this breakthrough moment. She needed his full attention, and he gave it willingly.

Several minutes passed before the heartrending weeping tapered off, her intermittent tears now accompanied by an occasional shuddering breath and sniffle. "I'm sorry."

The heartache he'd endured for years returned with the softly spoken words.

It's too much to ask of her.

How could he expect her to stay in a town associated with that much trauma?

He kissed her forehead, determined to set aside his disappointment and support her. Talking or guilting her into moving back to Creekside permanently would eventually backfire and she would leave again. "You have nothing to apologize for. Do you need a drink of water? There's probably a box of tissues around here somewhere too."

She clung to him, throwing him off-balance when he would've tried to stand and shift her to his chair. "I let you down the one time you really needed me. You were my best friend, and I ran away instead of helping you and trusting you to help me. I can never make up for that."

Had her apology been for what had happened when they were eighteen and not equipped to handle the horrors of a parent with cancer and another who'd failed his flesh and blood every day of her life?

If he had only a miniscule chance with her, he would seize it. What other choice did he have? "There were extenuating circumstances. For both of us. We can't change the past, but we can overcome it and right the real wrong. We deserve to be happy. Together."

The glasses did nothing to hide her red-rimmed eyes, a testament to how deeply she'd been hurt. In spite of her pain, the palpable emotion that glowed there made his pulse race and gave him hope. "I love you. How soon can we get married?"

EPILOGUE

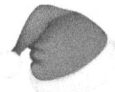

RING. MARRIAGE LICENSE. BRIDE.

Sven adjusted the fluffy white beard covering his jaw as he escorted Christy the short distance from the Creekside Town Hall to the gazebo in the park. Fresh snow dusted the sidewalk, the ground, and the wedding venue with its holiday decorations. The sun peeked out from between the icy clouds, making everything sparkle.

Magical.

Just like waking up next to her this morning.

His daughter, his parents, and the mayor waited for him and the love of his life at the bottom of the ramp. At least half the residents of his hometown surrounded the wooden structure where the high school band had played holiday songs at the Claus for a Cause festival last night. Some stood, but most sat in folding camp and lawn chairs. Bruce Springsteen and the E Street Band currently performed "Santa Claus is Coming to Town" through the sound system a local DJ had offered for what had been billed as a last-minute vow renewal of the couple from the North Pole.

Her gloved hand tucked in his, Mrs. Claus snuggled closer. "I can't believe Brenna pulled this off."

He huffed out a low laugh. "She's an expert at talking people into doing things for a good cause."

Within an hour of his text announcing his and Christy's engagement, his daughter had convinced the county clerk to issue a marriage license at four o'clock on a Saturday afternoon and then planned the entire event. The wedding of Santa and Mrs. Claus quickly evolved into a community affair to extend one of the most successful fundraisers in the town's history.

He didn't care that the whole thing had become a public spectacle. At the end, the woman he'd loved forever would be his wife.

Finally.

She suddenly slowed beside him, sending his insides spinning. "What was the deep breath for? Are you having second thoughts?"

The combination of the questions and her cautious tone stopped him in his tracks. He turned, cradled her face in his palms, and touched his chilly lips to hers. Warmth surged through his veins. "No second thoughts. Just impatient to hear you say I do. I've waited a long time for this."

"Okay." She rose on her tiptoes and shared another kiss with him. "Let's hurry."

He wanted to reassure her, especially after a flicker of insecurity flashed in her eyes, but moving the ceremony along was the best way to show how much he adored her. Grasping her hand in his again, he walked with her to the gathering and aimed a curt nod at the mayor.

The song ended and she opened a small book, announcing she was ready to begin the show. "Welcome, everyone. I'm honored to preside over a very special wedding today. The

Clauses have chosen to renew their marriage vows in our humble town."

As the mayor launched into a monologue about love withstanding the test of time, his daughter grinned up at him, without a doubt gloating over the results of her efforts to manipulate his love life. She'd admitted to playing matchmaker between him and the new friend she'd met a week and a half ago.

He hadn't needed her kick in the ass to fall madly in love with an occupational therapist who was supposed to be in town for only a few weeks to a month. The woman had owned his heart for more than three decades.

"Santa and Mrs. Claus will be reciting their own vows." The mayor gestured for Sven to go first.

Facing his bride, he held both of her hands in his and kept his voice low so none of the little ears in the audience would accidentally discover their true identities. "Christy, I've loved you almost my whole life, since the very first time I saw you. You were my best friend before I knew what my feelings meant. I treasured every second of the time we spent together as friends, as lovers, as soulmates. In all the years we were apart, you lived on in my heart. Now you're here again, and I can breathe and feel and hope. I can't wait to share the rest of my days and nights with you as your husband."

She squeezed his fingers, and a tear trickled toward her mouth unchecked. "Sven, you're my rock. You've been by my side through so many hardships, always holding me up when I thought I would fall, and you never let me push you away. The world dimmed when I didn't have you to lean on. Knowing you're here with me gives me the strength to face my fears and let love guide me. I've found happiness with you again and I'll cherish every day I get to be your wife."

After a glance at the book in her hands, the mayor closed

it, with her thumb marking her spot. "I understand you're exchanging rings. We'll keep this short since the weather's a bit nippy this morning. As you place the ring on each other's fingers, please recite the following. 'With this ring, I thee wed.'"

He nearly dropped his mittens, but they managed to slide on the matching set of wedding bands without a mishap.

"By the authority vested in me by the State of Ohio, I now pronounce you husband and wife. Mrs. Claus, you may—"

Lifting his bride off her feet, he sealed the deal with a kiss to rival the ones they engaged in under the mistletoe yesterday.

Raucous applause arose from their audience, and the rest of his family crowded in to congratulate him and his wife.

Warmth breath tickled his neck as she held on tight. "This is the best day of my life."

He kissed her again. "Mine too, Mrs. Claus."

THANKS FOR READING! IF YOU ENJOYED THIS STORY, PLEASE consider leaving a review on the retailer's website, BookBub, and/or Goodreads to help other readers find their next book!

Be sure to check out the rest of the books in The Naughty List series!

Are you ready for Brenna's story? Check out Roll With It!

ABOUT THE AUTHOR

Mellanie Szereto is the *USA Today* Bestselling Author of over sixty romcoms and contemporary romances, most with characters who have plenty of life experience like herself. Whether you call them older, seasoned, mature, experienced, or later-in-life protagonists, they deserve love too! Her stories are often set in small towns with quirky main characters, fun secondary casts, and lots of humor. She enjoys gardening, cooking, and baking—as well as hiking to work off the fruits of her labor—and incorporates food into all of her stories. She lives in an old farmhouse in rural Indiana with her husband of thirty-eight years.

Visit her website for more information about her books!